The Man Who Walked Like a Bear

The Man Who Walked Like a Bear

An Inspector Porfiry Rostnikov Novel

Stuart M. Kaminsky

Charles Scribner's Sons

New York

COPYRIGHT © 1990 BY STUART M. KAMINSKY

Charles Scribner's Sons
Macmillan Publishing Company
866 Third Avenue, New York, NY 10022
Collier Macmillan Canada, Inc.

This is a work of fiction. Names, characters, places, and incidents either are the product of the author's imagination or are used fictitiously. Any resemblance to actual events or persons, living or dead, is entirely coincidental.

Library of Congress Cataloging-in-Publication Data

Kaminsky, Stuart M.
    The man who walked like a bear: an Inspector Porfiry Rostnikov novel/
Stuart M. Kaminsky.
        p.   cm.
    ISBN 0-684-19023-0
    I. Title.
PS3561.A43M35   1990
813'.54—dc20   89-29082   CIP

10 9 8 7 6 5 4 3 2 1

Printed in the United States of America

M

To Michael, Patricia, Collin, **Cath,**
and Jane in Vancouver

"Clever! No, my dear fellow, that's clever! It is altogether too ingenious!"

"But why, why?"

"Simply because it is too neatly dovetailed . . . like a play."

"Oh!" Razumikhin began, but at that moment the door opened and a new personage came in, a stranger to everybody in the room.

Fyodor Dostoyevski,
Crime and Punishment

The Man Who Walked Like a Bear

Chapter One

Porfiry Petrovich Rostnikov sat in a rough but apparently sturdy wooden chair in ward three on the third floor of the September 1947 Hospital a little over twelve miles outside of Moscow. The September 1947 Hospital got its name from the fact that the city of Moscow was eight hundred years old in the year 1947. The citizens of Moscow had celebrated, cheered, drunk, and wept that their city had survived the war, the Nazis, the antirevolutionary forces.

People had hugged strangers in the street, and Porfiry Petrovich Rostnikov, an army veteran at age fifteen with a leg badly mangled in an encounter with a German tank, had sat on a stone bench in front of the Pashkov Mansion, which had become the Lenin Library. The leg had been patched, sawed, stretched, sewn, and supported, and Rostnikov had worked dutifully to use the appendage, which had almost been removed by an overworked and underexperienced young doctor in the field.

3

Stuart M. Kaminsky

Porfiry Petrovich Rostnikov allowed no one to see his pain, and not one of his superiors on the uniformed MVD traffic patrol knew of the pain he felt each day as he stood on some *prospekt* directing postwar traffic. It was that day in September 1947 that he met the woman who lay before him in Bed One of the hospital ward. Sarah had sat next to him on the bench, an old-fashioned kerchief around her head, her cheeks bright with life, her red hair curled over her forehead. She couldn't have been more than twelve years old. She had asked him if he was all right. He had replied that he was fine, and she had offered to share an apple with him. The rarity of an apple and the enormity of sharing such a gift with a stranger overwhelmed him, and he loved her, he loved her at that moment as he loved her at this moment. He had learned her name, her address, and had stayed away from her for six years, waited till she grew up. And then he had found her again.

Rostnikov shifted his weight in the sturdy chair and considered pulling out the battered American paperback mystery in his jacket pocket. His eyes met those of the young girl, Petra Toverinin, in Bed Two. Petra Toverinin was fourteen years old. Officially, she was there for gynecological complications. Unofficially, she was there for an abortion. Rostnikov had discerned this from no direct inquiry but from the guarded comments of the medical staff when he was present. Petra Toverinin was not pretty. She was thin. Her nose was too large and her hair too straggly and lifeless, but her eyes were large and blue and her lips carried a knowing smile, which she exchanged with Rostnikov whenever he came to visit his wife in Bed One. Petra Toverinin and Porfiry Petrovich Rostnikov shared a knowledge of life that needed no words and no conversation.

In Bed Three, however, there resided a woman named Irinia Komistok, heavy of heart, body, and thought. Irinia Komistok, somewhere over age sixty, whose heart had been abused by diet and discontent, had undergone one operation and was awaiting another.

"You are a policeman," Irinia Komistok informed Rostnikov, looking at him critically.

Rostnikov exchanged a knowing glance with Petra Toverinin, who put her head down on the pillow and turned away from the older woman in the third bed. Rostnikov looked at his sleeping wife and wondered if after the bandages were removed her red hair would grow back as bright as before, or if the gray would now take over. She was within a month of her fifty-fourth birthday. Dr. Yegeneva had assured him that Sarah would, barring complications, be home for her birthday.

"I am a policeman," Rostnikov confirmed, since Irinia Komistok had made a statement and not asked a question.

"I knew it," said the woman, who folded her hands in front of her over her blanket. "I knew it," she told the wall. "I could tell. My cousin Viktor was a policeman. A man named, named—I don't remember—lived downstairs from us in Volgograd. That was a few years ago. You know Volgograd?"

"No," said Rostnikov. Somewhere beyond the closed door of the ward a voice called out, distant, indistinct.

"Volgograd is beautiful," Irinia informed him, nodding her head. "I was a girl and the policeman looked at me with longing. I was a handsome girl. Not beautiful, mind

5

you. I'll make no great claims. I'm an honest woman. Why did you become a policeman?"

Petra looked at Rostnikov with sympathetic blue eyes.

"I don't know," said Rostnikov. "I had always wanted to be a policeman, perhaps because my parents had named me Porfiry Petrovich. He is the policeman in—"

"*Crime and Punishment,*" Irinia injected impatiently. "I am no uneducated Gypsy."

Another sound, deep, almost a growl beyond the ward's door.

"Have you noticed," Irinia Komistok said with a smile on her face that indicated no joy, "that time moves faster as you get older? When I was a girl, a year took forever, and now two years ago seems like last week."

"I have noticed," said Rostnikov.

And now the sound outside the ward's door could not be ignored. It approached in an echo, the corridor echo of a wounded animal. Petra Toverinin sat up afraid, her wide eyes wider than fear. Sarah stirred and shifted. Rostnikov leaned forward to touch her leg reassuringly through the blanket. Irinia Komistok seemed to have heard nothing. She spoke to the wall and saw ghosts until the door to the ward exploded open and banged with a roar into the wall. A large white sack hurtled through the door, crashed into the wall, and groaned.

An animal bellowed in the doorway, a huge, bearded, and quite naked animal. In the corner, the man who had been thrown against the wall tried to rise, groaned, and sank back to the floor. Irinia Komistok whimpered and Petra Toverinin scrambled painfully from her bed and climbed in next to Irinia, who hugged her. Sarah shifted her weight, and Rostnikov used the edge of the bed and the back of the sturdy wooden chair to stand. His back was to his wife's bed, and he faced the creature, who he knew was a man.

The man groaned and ambled forward like a great black bear Rostnikov had seen in the Moscow Circus the year before, a bear, he understood, who later attacked its trainer during a visit to Canada. The bear man slouched forward. Behind him Petra whimpered and Irinia comforted. The creature took a step toward Sarah's bed, and Rostnikov put up a hand.

The moment was fixed, frozen. The great creature, who stood a foot taller than the compact barrel of a policeman, let out a low growl and took two steps toward the window. Rostnikov stepped between the man and the window.

"No," Rostnikov said softly, firmly. "You are frightening these women."

The bearded creature blinked and looked around at the three women, noticing them for the first time.

"Sit in that chair," Rostnikov said, nodding at the chair in which he had been sitting.

The creature looked at the chair and then back at the policeman.

Porfiry Petrovich Rostnikov was, with good reason, known to his colleagues as the Washtub. There was nothing imposing about the fifty-seven-year-old man with one good leg and one very bad one, but Rostnikov had his passions—his books, his wife and son, his job, his weights. The creature before Rostnikov was at least fifteen years younger and at least fifty pounds heavier, in addition to which the man was obviously quite mad.

In the hall and far away footsteps echoed, clattered.

Someone was running. Voices were calling out in fear, and the man before Rostnikov heard them, too. He took another step toward the third-floor window. He was stomach to stomach with Rostnikov.

"Please," said the man, but it was less a human voice than the hum of a wounded dog.

"Sit," said Rostnikov gently.

The moment was absurd and Rostnikov felt the absurdity of himself and the creature in front of him. They were a bad joke. The man's breath smelled of black bread. The man's enormous penis brushed Rostnikov's chest.

"Please," the man insisted this time.

The footsteps were clambering closer.

"What?" Sarah said behind him, waking from her drugged sleep.

And this time the creature put his hairy hand on Rostnikov's shoulder, crunched his jacket in a great fist, and tried to shove the man in front of him to the side so he could get to the window. But the shorter man did not move.

"Please," bellowed the man, his head turned upward in near prayer and total panic.

"Sit," Rostnikov said firmly. "You are a man, not an animal. Sit."

The man looked at Rostnikov and raised both hands into tightfisted hammers. Someone stood in the doorway, but Rostnikov couldn't look. Petra screamed behind him. Rostnikov stepped forward quickly under the descending fists and locked his arms around the man's body at the waist. The massive man's fists thundered down on Rostnikov's back, but Rostnikov tightened his grip and lifted.

"Sit," Rostnikov repeated, but the man was thrashing and screaming and could hear nothing.

Rostnikov lifted him and stepped forward, forcing himself to put weight on his left leg, a weight that sent a familiar spasm of cold electricity through the policeman's body. He felt tears of pain in his eyes but took another step and placed the writhing creature in the chair.

Two white-uniformed men rushed forward and pinned the man's arms behind him, or attempted to. The creature threw one of the men from him. Rostnikov moved behind the chair and pushed the man down just as he was about to rise again. A stream of urine, dark and yellowish, shot forward from the man in the chair and barely missed one of the two uniformed men, who struck out with his closed fist at the nearly secured man in the chair, who kicked forward and sent the chair sliding back several feet.

"Leave him alone," Rostnikov said to the two uniformed men.

"Leave him . . ." one of the two uniformed men said, panting. Rostnikov couldn't tell which one spoke. He had not yet taken a look at them.

"Leave him," Rostnikov repeated firmly. The orderly who had spoken ignored him and reached out for the man. Rostnikov grabbed the orderly's wrist and repeated, "Leave him."

The orderly tried to pull away but couldn't free himself from the grasp. The man who walked like a bear tried to rise from the chair but Rostnikov firmly pushed him back down and said, "Sit."

Rostnikov looked up at the second orderly, a heavyset man with straight white-yellow hair who stood back and

folded his arms waiting to see what the little round madman planned to do with the enormous creature. Rostnikov
thought he detected a touch of intelligence or at least
cunning in the orderly, in contrast to the fear he felt in
the man whose wrist he held.

"Leave him, Anatoli," the man with white-yellow hair
said.

Rostnikov released the wrist, and Anatoli backed away
with a curse and moved to the wall to help the hurtled
orderly, who sat stunned and disoriented. The creature in
the chair kicked out with an animal growl and tried to
rise again, but Rostnikov could feel that there was less
desperation in his throes. Standing behind the chair,
Rostnikov put both hands on the man's shoulders, pushing him down and whispering, "You are a man, a man
with a name."

The man breathed heavily, clenched his teeth, and tried
to rise again. Rostnikov pushed him down.

"You are a man," Rostnikov repeated. "Behave like a
man, not an animal. What is your name? You are a man.
You have a name. What is your name?"

"His name is—" the orderly began.

"I asked *him*." Rostnikov stopped him. "I asked this
man who sits before me. What is your name? My name is
Porfiry. My wife in that bed is Sarah. In the bed in the
corner cowering in fear, thinking you are an animal and
not a man, are an old woman and a little girl. Let them
know you are a man."

"Bulgarin," rasped the man, going limp.

"Bul—" Rostnikov began.

"Bulgarin," the man repeated in a whisper so low that
only Rostnikov could hear.

"Bulgarin," Rostnikov repeated. "Can I release you now? Will you go calmly with these men?"

Bulgarin shook his head no.

"We can't sit here all morning, Bulgarin," said Rostnikov with a sigh. "I have work to do. The women need rest. These comrades have other patients to deal with. And you've made a mess in here. Someone will have to come clean it up."

"I'm sorry," said Bulgarin, his head going down.

"You want to be covered?" asked Rostnikov quietly.

Bulgarin nodded his head yes and Rostnikov nodded at the orderly with yellow-white hair. The orderly, amusement on his lips, stepped over to Petra's bed and pulled off a rumpled sheet. He threw the sheet to Rostnikov, who wrapped it around the now shivering giant.

"Go with them quietly, Bulgarin," Rostnikov said, releasing his hands from the man in the chair.

Bulgarin rose, wrapping the sheet closely to him, shaking. The three orderlies moved to the man's side and Bulgarin went gently with them to the door and then stopped suddenly and turned to Rostnikov.

"I had to," Bulgarin said, nearly weeping. "The devil came to devour the factory and I couldn't stop him. And he's found me here and has come to devour me."

"There is no devil, Bulgarin," Rostnikov said.

"Yes, there is," said Bulgarin, being led out the door and into the hall.

And Rostnikov thought but did not say that the world would be easier to deal with if there were a devil, if evil were clear and announced itself and wore the proper clothes or even disguised itself. In his thirty years of criminal investigation, Rostnikov had encountered only two criminals who admitted they were evil, and both of them were as mad as Bulgarin and not nearly as evil as dozens of criminals Rostnikov had encountered who defended their murders and rapes till the cell doors clanged closed at Lubyanka.

Rostnikov limped over to the door and closed it gently before he turned back into the room to face Sarah, whose white-turbaned head rested on the white pillow. Her face was pale, and there was a smile on her lips. The surgeon had assured Rostnikov that the tumor that had pressed against Sarah's brain had been removed and that she would gradually recover completely.

"I need rest, not entertainment, Porfiry Petrovich," she said.

Rostnikov moved to her side, touched her hand. Her hand was still cool. Not cold, but cool.

"He'll come back!" Petra cried from Irinia's bed.

Rostnikov looked over at the girl, who had less than three months ago been raped by a trio of drunks. Irinia was comforting her and herself.

"No," Rostnikov said. "He won't."

"He'll come back and—" Petra went on.

"He didn't come here to get you," Sarah said, taking her husband's stubby hand in both of hers. "He came in search of a window."

The door opened behind him and Petra let out a frightened squeal. Dr. Yegeneva, who had operated on Sarah, stepped in.

"They just told me," she began. "Are you all all right?"

Dr. Yegeneva adjusted her glasses and pushed her straight hair from her face. Dr. Yegeneva was somewhere in her thirties and, Rostnikov knew, had two children. "I don't know how that patient got up here. The mental ward is two flights up in the south section and—"

"I've got to get back to the city," Rostnikov said as the doctor moved to the far bed to comfort the girl and reassure the old woman.

"I wasn't afraid, Porfiry Petrovich," Sarah whispered.

"Thank you," he said.

"No, not just because of you," Sarah said, squeezing his hand. "I awoke from a dream I can't remember and I saw him there and there was such pain in his face. He reminded me of Benjamin."

Benjamin was Sarah's older brother, a large, dark, sullen, and suspicious man who had, from the first, been opposed to Sarah's having anything to do with Porfiry Petrovich. Sarah's father had died in the war. No one knew how or where. No one was even certain. He had gone, and when the war ended, he did not return. There were no records. But Benjamin had returned angry and bitter over the treatment he had received at the hands of the *goyim*, the non-Jews. He had received neither deserved promotions nor the small considerations that were common. He never considered that part of the fault might lie not in the anti-Semitism of his superiors but in his own attitude. Even under the best of situations, Sarah had admitted, Benjamin carried with him a rage so deep its roots could not be found.

And so Benjamin hated Porfiry Petrovich, and the reasons he gave were many. Porfiry Petrovich was not a Jew, and though there was not great profit in being Jewish in the Soviet Union, it was still safer to remain with your own people, the chosen people. In addition, Porfiry Petrovich was young, crippled, and a policeman. Porfiry

13

Petrovich remembered the last time he had seen Sarah's brother. Benjamin had warned Rostnikov that neither he nor his mother wanted Rostnikov to see Sarah again, that if he persisted, Benjamin would kill him.

Rostnikov had looked into the blue eyes of his future brother-in-law and believed him.

"I will marry Sarah," he had said. "And you will kill no one."

"We will see, police boy. We will all see," Benjamin had whispered.

And, indeed, they saw. Benjamin was killed in a street in front of the Aragvy Restaurant. Someone had insulted him, or Benjamin thought someone had insulted him. The someone had friends. This had not deterred Sarah's brother, who tried to strangle the offender while the offender's friends beat on the head of Benjamin Rosovsky with a convenient block of concrete from a nearby construction site.

———————

"I wasn't afraid," Sarah said. "I . . . be sure he is all right."

"I'll be sure," Rostnikov said, releasing his hands gently from her grip. "I'll be back tonight."

"You don't have to come back," she said. "I'll probably be sleeping."

They had gone through this patter for the past two weeks, and they both knew it as a ritual of reassurance.

"I'll see," Rostnikov said.

"Tell me something, Porfiry Petrovich, something of

the past," she said dreamily. "My thoughts move to the past in here, to my brother, my mother, to Iosef when he was a boy. Remember when he built that boat and it sank in the park? He was only a baby, and he jumped in after it and tried to swim."

Rostnikov smiled.

"I'm not good at sentiment," he said.

"You are fine with it," Sarah said. "Are you going to deny your ailing wife?"

"The week before we married," he said softly, "we went to Gorky Park with a loaf of bread and some herring in a bottle. You wore a blue dress and sweater and we drank kvass from a jar and you laughed at a joke I made about vegetables."

"I remember," Sarah said, closing her eyes.

"You were beautiful," he went on, almost to himself. "I should have borrowed Mikhail Sharinskov's camera, even if it wouldn't have captured the fire of your hair. But I . . ." and he could see she was asleep.

He leaned forward and kissed her forehead and then moved to the door, willing himself not to show the pain in his leg, knowing that he could not, ultimately, hide it from Sarah. All he could do was pretend so that she, too, could pretend.

So much is pretense, Rostnikov thought as he glanced at the young girl and the old woman across the room. He closed the door to the ward as Dr. Yegeneva moved past him and leaned over to look into Sarah's eyes.

The corridor walls of the September 1947 Hospital were uniformly gray, and the windows were all decorated with white linen curtains. The individual ward doors were heavy and closed, and Rostnikov had a dreamlike feeling, a feeling that he was wandering through a maze, an endless, echoing maze. Yes, it was the echo more than the seamless, uniform walls that gave him the feeling. He turned a corner, moving slowly, bidding his leg to respond, knowing how much he could coax out of it. A man in white and a heavyset woman came toward him, talking to each other loudly about some meeting. The man barely glanced at Rostnikov as they approached and passed.

Rostnikov found the administrator's office on the main floor after checking with a talkative, flighty woman at the central desk in front of the entrance to the hospital. The administrator's name, he discovered, was Schroeder, and the administrator, according to the woman at the desk, was a remarkably busy man. He had been on the job only a few days. The previous administrator had suddenly received a transfer to a very important position in the city.

Rostnikov knocked and entered when he heard a clear male voice call, "Come in."

The room was bright. A large window caught the morning sun and lit the cheerfully decorated room. There was a small white rug on the floor, an efficient and not uncomfortable-looking set of chairs around a low, round table, and a wooden desk behind which sat a pink-cheeked, robust man with short-cropped hair and a smile on his large lips. His suit was neatly pressed and he looked at Rostnikov like an indulgent priest.

"Yes?" the man asked eagerly.

"Comrade Schroeder?"

"Correct," said Schroeder, waiting for more.

"My name is Rostnikov. My wife is a patient of Dr. Yegeneva on the third floor."

"Sarah, brain tumor. Removed successfully. Prognosis excellent," said Schroeder. "I know each and every patient in this hospital. Eighty-five patients at present. Learned the essential information in three days."

"Admirable," said Rostnikov. "May I sit?"

"Please," said Schroeder.

Rostnikov sat and felt an instant easing as the weight left his throbbing leg.

"I want to ask you about another patient," Rostnikov said.

"Bulgarin, Ivan," Schroeder supplied.

"Yes. You've been informed, then, about the incident?"

Schroeder looked pleased with himself.

"I am responsible for all aspects of this hospital," he said. "I am constantly informed."

"Admirable," said Rostnikov.

Schroeder reached into his desk and withdrew a folder, which he opened and flattened before him.

"Bulgarin, Ivan, age . . . let me see. He will be forty-two next week. He has been here for six days. Fatigue, overwork. He is a foreman in the Lentaka Shoe Factory. Diagnosis is a bit complicated but, essentially, he suffered a mental breakdown caused by hard work, an unstable personality, and domestic difficulties. He has a wife and four children. I am assured by the staff that he will be ready for release and a productive return to society in less than a month, depending on his response to medication."

"You are most informative," said Rostnikov, trying to make eye contact with the administrator.

"You are a police officer," Schroeder said, closing the folder and looking up. "See, I even know that. Easy enough. It was in your wife's admission record."

"Who is paying for Comrade Bulgarin's hospitalization? Why wasn't he sent to a public hospital?"

Schroeder again looked at Rostnikov for an instant. "I'll be honest with you, Comrade. Bulgarin is a party member, not because of his political zeal but because he has relatives who are . . . well connected. I've said more than I should, but I expect I can trust to your discretion."

"Why?" Rostnikov asked again.

"I just—" Schroeder began in some confusion.

"Why do you expect you can trust to my discretion? You've never met me before, and I am a policeman."

"I don't . . . I . . . am I incorrect?"

"No," said Rostnikov. "What is Bulgarin's problem?"

"A breakdown. He—"

"No," Rostnikov interrupted again. "He appeared to have some delusion. What is the nature of that delusion? He said something about a devil devouring the factory."

Schroeder shrugged nervously and adjusted his tie.

"Who knows?" he said. "Devils, spacemen, talking animals, plots. We have a woman here who speaks to Karl Marx. Who knows with these? I can summon the physician assigned to his case."

"That won't be necessary," said Rostnikov, standing.

"You are in some physical distress?" said Schroeder, rising from his chair and proving to be considerably shorter than Rostnikov had thought.

"An ancient wound," said Rostnikov. "I thought I hid it reasonably well."

"You do," said Schroeder. "But remember, though I am not a physician, I have almost thirty years of experience with symptoms. Can I tell you anything else?"

"Your name is German," Rostnikov said, walking to the door.

"Yes, my parents moved to the Soviet Union before I was born. I can't even speak German."

"Thank you for your cooperation," said Rostnikov.

"Not at all," said Schroeder, coming out from behind the desk. "Such incidents are rare, very rare, and, besides, Bulgarin is quite harmless. I'm assured he is quite harmless. Your wife is quite safe."

"I wasn't concerned about her safety," said Rostnikov.

"Well, you know—"

And with that Rostnikov departed, closing the door behind him.

The morning was pleasant, cool, and the sky a bit threatening. Rostnikov reminded himself to take the umbrella the next day. He frequently reminded himself, but invariably forgot unless Sarah was home and caught him before he left the apartment.

There was an MVD car, a not reliable 1974 Zhiguli, waiting for him in front of the hospital. Officially Rostnikov was a member of the MVD, the uniformed and nonuniformed police responsible for maintaining order, preventing crime, and pursuing lawbreakers for all but political and economic offenses. Political and economic offenses were the mission of the KGB, the Komityet Gosudarstvennoy Bezopasnosti, or State Security Agency. And Rostnikov had discovered when still a young policeman that any crime was political or economic in the Soviet Union if the KGB chose to see it as such, even the beating of a wife by her husband or the murder of the husband by a beaten wife.

Rostnikov climbed into the back of the car. He did not

drive. He knew how to do it and had done it many years ago. The skill was probably still there, but the desire had never glowed. Driving was a distraction. Rostnikov's superior, Colonel Snitkonoy, the Gray Wolfhound, had insisted on Rostnikov's taking the car and uniformed driver, and Rostnikov had not refused.

"I want you back as quickly as possible," the Wolfhound had said, standing tall, hands folded behind his back, brown uniform perfectly pressed and glowing with medals. "There is much to be done, and I can't afford to have you wasting your time on buses. You understand."

"Completely," Rostnikov had said.

And so he sat in the backseat of the car, heading back to Moscow along the Volokolamsk Highway while the young woman driver made no conversation. Rostnikov always sat in the back of the car, though the custom was to sit in the front to keep from looking like an elitist. Rostnikov had no concern about such accusations, and the distance from the driver relieved them both of the obligation to carry on an unwanted conversation.

Schroeder, he was sure, had been lying. Rostnikov wasn't sure about how much lying he had done, but he had lied. The administrator had been too ready, too cooperative. The busy administrator had been sitting there waiting for Rostnikov, possibly expecting him. And Schroeder had been sweating. There was nothing wrong with sweating. Many people sweated in the presence of a policeman, even if they were guilty of no crime. In fact, it was almost impossible in the Soviet Union to be innocent of all crimes, since the definition of crime included intent. Someone could be guilty of thinking improperly. Yes, things had changed recently. People talked of *demokra-*

tizatsiya, democratization, but those things could change back again with a bullet, a quiet coup. It wasn't that Schroeder sweated but that he did not take the handkerchief out of his pocket and wipe his brow. It had been important to Schroeder to make it seem that he was not nervous. Something was being hidden. It might be anything, from illegal purchase of medical supplies to the use of banned medications, but Rostnikov didn't think so. He was convinced that it had something to do with Bulgarin, the man who walked like a bear.

Rostnikov pulled the worn paperback from his pocket and turned to the page where Carella had just learned about the headless magician.

Chapter Two

The woman sat looking straight ahead, her coat still buttoned, her mouth firmly set. She was somewhere in her late forties and, Sasha was sure, wanted to be thought of as a stylish modern person. He discerned this because of the woman's short haircut, her use of makeup, and the stylish if somewhat worn imitation leather coat she wore.

She was also a challenge. She had been sitting silently in the small interrogation room of Petrovka for more than fifteen minutes and had said nothing after informing the uniformed officer at the entrance that she had something of importance to say to a policeman. Petrovka consists of two ten-story L-shaped buildings on Petrovka Street. It is modern, imposing utilitarian, and very busy. It is a place most Muscovites avoid. Often citizens will come through the doors determined to be heard and seen, only to change their mind at the sight of the humorless young officers carrying dark automatic weapons. But this woman, though afraid, had persisted.

Sasha Tkach had the unfortunate luck to be seated at his desk opposite Zelach when the woman was brought up. Sasha was usually successful with reluctant witnesses. He was handsome if a bit thin and looked much younger than his twenty-nine years. His hair fell over his eyes, and he had an engaging habit of throwing his head back to clear his vision. He also had a rather large space between his upper teeth, which seemed to bring out the maternal response in most women, but this woman, whose identification confirmed that her name was Elena Vostoyavek, did not respond to Sasha's charms and, truth be told, Sasha had other things on his mind, particularly the fight he had had that very morning with his wife, Maya, over whether Sasha's mother, Lydia, would be moving with them and the baby to the new apartment. It had been an unusually difficult fight because Lydia, deaf as she was, had been in the next room and might hear.

Sasha did not need this silent challenge before him. He needed a simple day of desk work, distracting, absorbing desk work without human contact. He had a pile of reports to write. He longed to write those reports, to lose himself in the routine of those reports, and so he decided to charm the reluctant woman.

"Can I get you some tea?" Sasha said, leaning close to her and smiling.

No answer.

"This must be difficult for you," he went on, speaking softly, intimately. "Whatever it is you have to tell us must be important, and we appreciate your sense of responsibility. Too many citizens walk away from their responsibility."

The woman did not look at him. He pulled up a chair and sat directly in her line of vision. Inspector Rostnikov had told him there would be moments like this when they moved to special assignments in the MVD. They—Rostnikov, Tkach, and Emil Karpo—had handled important cases, murders, grand theft when they were with the procurator general's office, which under Article 164 of the Constitution of the USSR is empowered to exercise "supreme power of supervision over the strict and uniform observance of laws by all ministries, state committees and departments, enterprises, institutions and organizations, executive-administrative bodies of local Soviets of People's Deputies, collective farms, cooperatives, and other public organizations, officials, and citizens." The procurator general's office was a place of great prestige and, as long as its mission did not conflict with the KGB, great power. But Rostnikov had, once too often, incurred the wrath of the KGB and had been demoted, assigned to the staff of Colonel Snitkonoy, whose duties were largely ceremonial.

Tkach and Karpo, already under suspicion because of their loyalty to Rostnikov, had been given the opportunity to join him. The opportunity had no alternatives, and Tkach had accepted it gladly, though at moments like this he longed for a good murder.

"You're married?" Tkach said. "Your ring is very interesting."

Elena Vostoyavek did not answer.

"We know a little about you," he said, patting the sheet of paper that had been handed to him just before he entered the room with the woman.

"Your husband died several years ago after a prolonged illness. Is that correct?"

Tkach knew it was correct. The woman did not answer.

"You have a son, Yuri, who is . . . nineteen years old. He works at the Central Telegraph Office. Is that correct?"

No response.

"Elena, I'll be honest with you. I need your help here. I have a lot of paperwork to do, and I'm expected to get a statement from you. If I don't, my superiors will consider me incompetent. It will count against me. I have a wife, a child. You don't want that to happen? You have a son. My mother would be broken if I lost my position here. You understand what I'm saying?"

No response. Sasha sighed and threw back his head to clear his eyes. There was a challenge here, and he was not meeting it. The woman was not just being stubborn. He could sense that. She had something to say, but something was keeping her from it. He needed the key that would open her mouth.

"All right," he said, standing, suddenly louder than he had been. "I've been patient with you, but my patience has ended. We are busy here. I am busy, and you are taking valuable time from my investigative schedule. According to the law, you can now be tried for interference with police procedure. I am prepared, if I must, to bring such charges against you. You have five more of my minutes before I call an end to this and make a criminal charge."

A tear formed in the corner of Elena Vostoyavek's right eye. Sasha sighed and handed her the handkerchief Maya had ironed for him that morning even as they had fought. The silent woman took the handkerchief, touched it to her eye, and delicately blew her nose before handing the handkerchief back.

Sasha stuffed the handkerchief in his pocket, folded his arms across his chest, and sat back against the table behind him. The woman sniffled several times but didn't seem to notice as Sasha announced the passage of each minute.

"Five," he said, standing. "It is time to place charges against you."

He had no intention of placing charges. He would usher her to the front door, inform the guard that she was not to be allowed back into the building, and then go back to his desk and write a report on the encounter. He looked forward to that report.

It was clear the woman would not speak. She wanted magic, a miracle, for him to know what she wanted without her having to say it. At that moment the door to the interrogation room opened and a tall figure entered. The door was at Sasha's back, but he could tell from the silent woman's eyes who had entered. Elena's eyes raised to take in the figure, and then the eyes widened and the mouth opened. She composed herself almost before the door had closed, but the look on her face was familiar to Tkach.

Emil Karpo stepped forward next to Sasha. Karpo was over six feet tall, lean, with dark, thinning hair and pale skin that contrasted with the black suit he wore. He looked corpselike, and his dark eyes were cold and unblinking. When he spoke, his voice was an emotionless monotone. He had been known in his early police career as the Tatar, but twenty years of fanatical pursuit of enemies of the state had earned him the nickname of the

Vampire among his colleagues. The name seemed particularly appropriate when a peculiar look crept into Karpo's eyes, and at those moments even those who had worked with him for years avoided him. Only Rostnikov knew that the look was caused by severe migraine headaches, headaches that Emil Karpo never acknowledged. There was also a peculiar lilt of Karpo's body as he moved forward, a lilt caused by a vulnerable left arm that had been repeatedly damaged in the line of duty and only recently repaired by surgery.

"She won't speak," Sasha said with a sigh without looking at his pale companion.

Karpo nodded, his eyes fixed on the face of the woman who was doing her best not to be afraid of this new presence. But her best was far from good enough. Karpo picked up the information sheet from the table, read it quickly, and shifted his eyes to the face of the woman in the chair, who failed to avert her eyes in time and found them locked on those of the Vampire.

"Why are you here, Elena Vostoyavek?" he said.

"My-my-my son," she answered dryly.

Sasha put his hand to his forehead and shook his head.

"What about your son?" Karpo went on insistently.

"I think," she said, pulling her coat more tightly around her in spite of the heat of the room, "I think he is planning to do something very bad. I heard him talking to someone—a girl, I think—on the phone."

"Something bad?" Karpo prompted.

"Something bad," she repeated.

"And what is this bad thing?" asked Karpo patiently.

The woman looked at the two policemen and then at the wall.

"What is this thing?" Karpo repeated with less patience.

"Kidnapping," she said softly. "I think he is planning to kidnap Andrei Morchov or worse. He mentioned Comrade Morchov several times."

"The Politburo member?" asked Sasha.

The woman nodded her head and looked down at the floor.

"Why are you telling us?" asked Sasha, certain now that he would not be getting to his paperwork and thoughts this day.

"To stop him," she said. "If you tell him you know what he is planning, thinking, he won't be able to do it, don't you see? No crime will have been committed. It's just a crazy ... Yuri is not a bad boy. He just gets ... well, he's not really a boy anymore, not really. But a mother—you understand? You have children?"

"No," said Karpo.

The word *conspiracy* came into Sasha's thoughts. If her son were guilty of planning a kidnapping, especially the kidnapping of an important member of the Politburo, that was a crime whether he succeeded or not, even if the plan were only something he mentioned once and never planned to carry out.

"You'll talk to him, stop him, frighten him," she said, looking directly at Karpo and reaching out to touch his hand. Karpo withdrew his hand before the contact was made and stood erect. "I'm sure you could frighten him."

"We will stop him," said Karpo.

———————

Stuart M. Kaminsky

Bus number 43, driven by Boris Trush on the 75 route, pulled over in front of Sokolniki Recreation Park at eleven-twelve in the morning. Boris announced the stop and opened the doors. Four of his passengers got off, leaving only a half-asleep man with a cap pulled over his eyes and an old couple arguing in the rear.

Boris had a hangover. He wanted to be home in the dark or immersed in warm water. Before all this reform, this *perestroika*, economic restructuring, and *glasnost*, openness, all this change, a man could have a hangover, a man could get drunk, a man had reason to drink. Now there were signs posted all over the city saying drinking was subversive, that drinking undercut the very fabric of the revolution. First they had raised the drinking age to twenty-one. That had been a good idea. Then Gorbachev had increased the price of vodka from four and a half rubles to ten rubles a liter. That had been a bad idea. And there were more bad ideas. Cutting the hours of State stores that sold alcohol was one.

Soon, Boris Trush thought, they will be making us embarrassed about smoking the way they are in the United States. What will be left when they take away the minor vices of the overweight and the middle-aged? Boris was, clearly, in a very dark mood when the two men climbed onto the bus, dropped their five kopecks in the box, and tore off their tickets.

Boris did not look at the faces of the men. He barely noticed that one was wearing jeans and a dark jacket, and the other was older and also wore sunglasses. The young man was like all the other young people, like his own sister's son, Vladimir. Young people wanted to look like Frenchmen or Americans or even Japanese. Where was

32

their pride? Boris had heard that Soviet watches were in great demand in France. He pulled away from the curb and into the light late-morning traffic.

"What is your name?" a voice said behind Boris.

Boris looked up into his mirror into the dark lenses of the glasses of the young man. Beyond the young man who spoke to him Boris could see the second man, an older man in a long coat talking to the old couple in the back.

"Don't talk to the driver," Boris said.

"Hey, Comrade," the young man said. "I'm just trying to make things easier."

Boris's head ached. The young man in the mirror talking to him had long blond hair and needed a shave. He looked undernourished and nervous.

"Sit down," Boris said.

The young man sat behind Boris and looked out the window.

"Stop here," the young man said.

"There is no stop here," said Boris. "No stop. No talking. I'll announce the stops."

A light rain had begun. Boris turned on his windshield wipers.

"Stop here," the young man said evenly and reached over to touch something against Boris's neck. Boris, startled, almost lost control of the bus. He did move slightly into the outer lane, but there was no traffic.

"You crazy lunatic," Boris said with a growl, pulling over to the curb. "Get off my—"

And with that Boris Trush stopped, for at this point he turned his head and saw that the thing that had touched his neck was the barrel of a pistol in the young man's hand.

"You know what this is?" the blond young man said.

"A gun," Boris said, quietly blaming Gorbachev for this moment. If it weren't for Gorbachev, Boris could have called in to his supervisor this morning, made the old excuse, which would have been understood, and Boris could have been home in a dark room with his pain. But that was no longer acceptable. Everyone wanted to show sobriety, zeal, support, a new beginning. Not only did it make Boris Trush sick, it now also showed signs of possibly killing him.

"It's not just a gun, Comrade," the young man whispered. "Open the doors."

Boris opened the doors and looked up in the mirror to see the old couple being escorted off the bus by the man who had gotten on with the gunman.

"He told them there's a problem with the bus," the young man whispered. "You wanted to know about this?"

The young man held the gun out so Boris could get a better look at it. Boris did not want to know.

"This is a Stechkin," the young man whispered almost lovingly. "The slide-mounted safety catch has three positions: safe, repetition, and automatic. When I move the catch like this and clip this wooden holsterstock to the butt, the Stechkin is no longer a pistol but a submachine gun with a twenty-shot box. Nice, huh?"

The man in the long coat moved forward with no sense of urgency and shook the shoulder of the dozing man with the cap over his eyes.

"Hey," the man in the long coat said. "Last stop."

As Boris watched in his mirror, the dozing man roused himself, pushed his cap back with irritation, and looked out the window. He was a burly man, a laborer of some kind, Boris was sure, for the man was a regular on Boris's route and frequently got on the bus with grimy hands and face.

"It's not the last stop," the laborer grumbled and pulled the cap back over his eyes.

"Bus is down," the long-coated man said, jostling the laborer's shoulder again.

This time the laborer pulled his hat off and grabbed the neck of the long-coated man standing over him.

"Who the hell are you?" the laborer growled, looking around the bus for the first time.

The young blond man standing next to Boris sighed, pushed his dark glasses back on his nose, and turned. Calmly, the young man raised his gun and fired. Boris jumped and yelped like a puppy, as if it were he who had been shot. The tin-can rattle of the shot echoed through Boris's aching head as he turned in his seat and saw the long-coated man push away the blood-spattered body of the laborer, who wore a quite surprised look on his face.

"Close the doors," the young man said, looking outside to see if anyone had heard or seen what had happened. The old couple who had been evicted from the bus were half a block away. They turned, looked back.

"Wave at them," the young man said.

Boris waved.

"Now close the doors."

And Boris closed the doors.

"The Stechkin is unreliable," the young man said conversationally. "Too big as a pistol. Too light as a submachine gun. It makes big holes but . . . You never told me your name."

"Boris, Boris Trush. I have a wife and four children."

The man from the rear of the bus had now joined them. The young man adjusted his sunglasses and turned to him.

"This is Boris Trush. Comrade Trush says he has a wife and four children. I think Boris may be lying just a little bit. I think he may not have four children. He looks like too good a citizen to have so many children. I think Comrade Trush is afraid."

"Enough," said the older man in the long coat.

Boris wanted to remove his cap. He knew his nearly hairless scalp was drenched with sweat that would soon be burning his eyes. He looked up at his mirror into the shaded eyes of the older man and shuddered. The man looked like an older, more conservative version of the young man with the gun, but the older man held no gun in his hand. He held a very narrow piece of dark metal pipe.

"You have a picture of your family, Boris?" the young man teased.

"I . . . not with me."

"Enough," said the older man.

"But, Boris—" the young man began but never finished.

The older man brought the metal pipe down with a ringing clang against the steel change box next to Boris, who pulled in his breath and began panting.

"We have work," the older man said. "Get in the back and keep your eyes open."

The young man nodded and backed away.

"You'll have to forgive him," said the older man quietly to Boris as he tapped the metal pipe into the palm of his left hand. "He's young and nervous. He's never done anything like this."

"I forgive him," said Boris, thinking that yes, oh, he certainly was going to wet his pants. "What are you going to do?"

"Steal this bus," said the man. "Now, if you will drive where I tell you, there is a chance—a slight chance, I must admit, but a chance—that you will live long enough to tell this story to the police."

Chapter Three

Gentlemen, there is a cancer in our midst."

Colonel Snitkonoy, the Gray Wolfhound, made his pronouncement and paused to watch its effect upon his senior staff. The Wolfhound, slender, resplendent in his perfectly pressed brown uniform, medals glittering, had paused, hands behind his back, white mane finely brushed back, head erect.

The Wolfhound headed the MVD's Bureau of Special Events. The MVD consisted of the uniformed and ununiformed police who directed traffic, faced the public, and were the first line of defense against crime. Everyone, with the possible exception of Colonel Snitkonoy, knew that the Gray Wolfhound headed the Special Events Bureau because he looked as if he had been cast for the role. His real job was to appear at public events, present medals, make patriotic speeches at factories, and handle criminal investigations that no other bureau wanted.

Stuart M. Kaminsky

Before his transfer to the Wolfhound's staff, Porfiry Petrovich Rostnikov had been a senior inspector in the procurator general's office in Moscow. The procurator general is appointed for a seven-year term, the longest of any Soviet official. The procurator general is responsible for sanctioning arrests, supervising investigations, executing sentences, and supervising trials. Now, following any inquiry, or *doznaniye,* Rostnikov would have to turn over his information to the procurator general's office if the case were of sufficient importance to go to trial.

And now Rostnikov, having arrived late at the morning administrative meeting, sat doodling as the Gray Wolfhound stood waiting for the appropriate response from the three men seated around the wooden table in his large office. Rostnikov looked down pensively at the credible drawing of a bear he was working on. On Rostnikov's right sat Pankov, the ever-frightened Pankov, a near-dwarf of a man with thinning hair who served as the colonel's assistant and who always appeared in public at the colonel's side to present a startling contrast and further bring out the impressive figure of the Wolfhound. Pankov, rumpled, unkempt, confused, was treated with great respect by his superior. The third man at the table was Major Grigorovich, who sat three seats down, a solid, uniformed block of a man in his middle forties who was ever alert and ever prepared to support the Wolfhound's philosophy of life in the clear hope of taking over when the colonel made the inevitable mistake that would bring him down.

"Pankov," the Wolfhound said, turning his eyes to the frightened little man.

"Yes, Colonel, a cancer," said Pankov.

"Go on, Pankov," the Wolfhound said attentively.

Pankov's professional life was totally dependent on the continued success of the Wolfhound. And yet Pankov always harbored the hope that he might survive if and when the great man stepped down or was stepped upon. To do that he had to keep from offending Grigorovich, who might find him useful enough to retain, and not annoy Rostnikov, who might turn in a report on his incompetence.

"Crime," Pankov began. "The criminals. There is too much, a cancer."

"Too much?" said the Wolfhound.

Pankov's eyes turned to Rostnikov, who continued to write in his little book, and Grigorovich, whose eyes met Pankov's with no sign of sympathy.

"I mean," said Pankov, "any crime is too much. The figures show that crime is being reduced significantly and—"

"Crime has increased in the past year," said Snitkonoy. "Grigorovich, the Interior Ministry report."

Grigorovich slowly reached forward and opened the notebook in front of him. He cleared his throat and said in his deepest and most serious voice, "Assaults, robberies, and theft increased by twenty-five to forty-four percent in the past year. Murders were up fourteen percent and rapes five percent throughout the Soviet Union. The overall crime rate increased in the past year by seventeen point eight percent. Violent crimes, street crimes, thefts are up even more."

"I did not have access to this information," Pankov pleaded.

"It was published in *Izvestiya*," said Grigorovich.

Rostnikov thought of the old joke that there is no

pravda (truth) in *Izvestiya* and no *izvestiya* (news) in *Pravda.* That had changed quite a bit in the past four years, but not completely.

Pankov sat back defeated, wondering if his cousin in Leningrad would let him work in his furniture store.

"It is better to know the reality of things," the Wolfhound said, resuming his pacing. "Because then our level of security will be clearer, as well as the tasks and the problems that we face.

"Criminals are preying on newly formed cooperative businesses. Street fighting among rival gangs of youths has reached murderous levels right in our city. Some people have claimed that General Secretary Gorbachev's political and social reforms, which have relaxed state controls, are to blame for this grave new crime wave."

The Wolfhound turned suddenly on his staff. Pankov looked away, defeated. Grigorovich sat ready to respond, and Rostnikov paused in his drawing to look up. Snitkonoy's eyes fell on Rostnikov.

"According to the Ministry report," said Rostnikov, "there were fifty-seven crimes for every hundred thousand people in the Soviet Union, while the United States in a comparable period had five thousand, five hundred fifty crimes for every hundred thousand people."

"Yes, yes, yes," agreed Snitkonoy, "but what difference does it make to us? We know the Americans distort their crime figures. It must be even worse there than they are willing to admit."

"Fortunately," said Rostnikov, "we can place our complete trust in the figures supplied to us by the Interior Ministry."

"And we will redouble our efforts," said Snitkonoy.

"We will not rest. What do we have in progress and what is new? Pankov?"

Pankov pulled himself together and flattened the morning report in front of him.

"Visit from the trade delegation from the American United State of Illinois," said Pankov. "The Trade Ministry would like you to join the minister for lunch with the American today. I've taken the liberty of scheduling it. Um, traffic accident report is up again. Investigators Karpo and Tkach have a possible crank report of a boy who says he wants to kidnap a Politburo member, but I doubt that it is worth serious consideration. A distraught mother simply overheard a conversation she almost certainly misunderstood. Next, the Central Bus Authority reports a missing vehicle, the assault squad—"

"Enough," said Snitkonoy. "Pass it around. Porfiry Petrovich, have your people check on the kidnap report and the missing vehicle. Grigorovich, coordinate the accident investigation report. Any questions?"

The colonel, all around the table knew, had been aware of the lunch with Americans for months and had been looking forward to it and practicing his English with Rostnikov. The duties the colonel had just assigned were the routine responsibilities of the men to whom they had been assigned. In each case, the investigation or report would be taken over by a higher agency if anything came to the surface to indicate something beyond the routine. Rostnikov knew that if he wanted to complete an investigation he had to move quickly and report slowly or risk losing the assignment.

"Gentlemen, to work," said the Wolfhound, moving to the window to look out at the streets of Moscow.

The three men rose, Rostnikov more slowly than the others.

"Porfiry Petrovich, you will remain for a moment."

Grigorovich gathered his papers and hurried militarily to the doorway through which Pankov had already scurried. When the door was closed, the colonel moved to his desk and said, in English, "The weather in your state, I understand, is conducive to the growing of corn."

"It is," said Rostnikov in English.

"Fine." The Wolfhound signed some documents and went on in English, "Perhaps a reciprocity of agricultural and machine tools will be an eventuality between your state and our proper representatives."

"It is a possibility, Colonel," said Rostnikov.

The Wolfhound turned with a smile and continued in English, "How is the progression of your wife, Inspector?"

"She is progressing, Colonel. Thank you."

"A good wife is a stone to hold one down," said the Wolfhound.

"A rock to rely on," Rostnikov corrected gently.

"*Da*," the Wolfhound said seriously, returning to Russian. "A rock to rely on. The American idiom contradicts itself and is often difficult to fathom."

"Yes," agreed Rostnikov.

"The Russian language, in contrast, has a singular clarity of meaning." And then in English, "I then bid you good morning."

The Wolfhound returned his pen to the desk and looked up at Rostnikov. Once when they were preparing a list of names of MVD officers to escort a visiting policeman from Kiev, Rostnikov had offered the colonel a pencil so they could make adjustments in the list if they wished to do so. The colonel had smiled and continued to use his pen, saying, "I never use a pencil. I haven't the time to change my mind."

"Good morning," Rostnikov replied and went through the door of the Wolfhound's den and out to meet the day.

<hr>

Sasha Tkach had one hour for lunch. His wife, Maya, had asked to meet him in front of the memorial chapel on Kuibyshev Street, directly across from the Ploschad Nogina Metro station. Sasha crossed Kirov Street, moved past the Dzerzhinsky Metro station, and hurried down the Serov passage past the Polytechnical Museum to Kuibyshev Street.

He pulled the collar of his jacket down now that the light rain had ended. He crossed the street and saw his wife and baby daughter at a bench. Maya saw her husband crossing the street and turned the baby, who was standing in front of her holding on to the bench. Pulcharia was just beginning to stand, though she needed something or someone to hold on to. She saw Sasha as he approached and began to wave; the tassels on the blue knit sweater she was wearing bobbed with her zealous wave, and Sasha smiled at his daughter's open, toothless grin.

"It's *at'e'ts*, your father," Maya said, and she, too, smiled as Sasha leaned over to kiss them. They had been married for almost three years now and the baby was nearly a year old. It seemed to Sasha that they had been married much longer. He could not remember the details, the day-to-day rituals of his life before this woman and child.

"I haven't long," Sasha said, taking a sandwich from Maya.

There was at least the hope of sun now.

"What we can get, we take," she said, tearing off a piece of bread and putting it into Pulcharia's waiting mouth.

Maya's words resonated with a Ukrainian accent that Sasha found exotic. He knew what she wanted to talk about, and he knew that it couldn't be avoided.

"Lydia," Maya said.

"Yes," said Sasha with a sigh.

They would soon be moving from their apartment into a slightly larger one. The move had come about after a complex series of trades arranged by a friend of Lydia's from childhood. Their apartment would go to an old couple and their daughter. The old couple, in turn, would give their centrally located apartment over to an accountant for the Ts UM department store, where Maya worked part time. Sasha and Maya would then get the accountant's apartment, which was larger than their own though farther from the city. Everyone got something they wanted from the trade and lost something. The old couple got a slightly larger apartment but gave up their proximity to the central city. The accountant would be close to his work, and Sasha and Maya would have more room. The problem was Sasha's mother, Lydia. The nearly deaf Lydia still worked at the Ministry of Information as a file clerk, but she would be retired in a little over a year. Sasha was well aware that his mother was difficult to live with under the best of circumstances, and having her around constantly was trying even for her son. They had spent their entire married life sharing the apartment with Lydia.

"You'll have to tell her, Sasha," Maya said gently.

The baby pulled at Sasha's trousers and he handed her a piece of bread. Maya took the bread from the baby and tore it into smaller pieces before handing her a single piece.

"She's my mother," Sasha said, looking into his wife's dark eyes. "How does one tell his mother she can't live with him? Especially my mother. Could you do it to your mother? Besides, the apartment is really hers. We moved in with her."

"My mother wouldn't want to live with us," Maya said. "But could I do it? Yes, if I had to. And we have to, Sasha."

Sasha could hear his mother's voice vividly, sharply in his mind. He almost turned on the bench to look for her. A passing shopper smiled at Pulcharia, who offered the woman a piece of her bread.

"She arranged for the new apartment," Sasha reminded his wife, who reached over and brushed the hair from his eyes.

"And she gave birth to you and you love her and she drives you mad and she drives me mad," Maya said gently. "Your aunt wants her. You aunt is lonely."

"They don't get along," sighed Sasha. "You know that."

"Lydia doesn't get along with anyone."

"She gets along with you," he said, reaching over to pick up the baby, who was reaching out to him.

"I get along with her," Maya corrected.

"She has to be told," he said, kissing his daughter.

"She'll be one bus from us," said Maya, touching his hand. "She can come twice a week. We'll probably get along better with her."

"I'll tell her tonight," Sasha said, looking around at a pair of old women walking arm in arm down the sidewalk.

Maya leaned over to kiss him on the cheek. Her kiss was warm, and he smiled.

"After all," he said to the baby, "what can your grand-mother do to me?"

Pulcharia, who was named for Lydia's mother, decided her father had made a joke and she laughed, but her father did not laugh with her.

Chapter Four

Zelach wore his most attentive look. His lips were tight and his eyes narrowed and fixed on Rostnikov. Zelach tried to hold his thick body erect in the chair, but it refused to cooperate, requiring Zelach to expend great amounts of limited will and mental resources on the effort. Such a concentration and expenditure of effort to juggle his air of attention while at the same time actually listening to Rostnikov was a greater task than his body was equipped for. Zelach settled for a look of greater and greater concentration in the hope that he would either deceive his colleagues and superiors or something magical would take place. Adding to his discomfort was the fact that Zelach was very hungry and lunchtime had come and gone.

Zelach had neither wit nor talent, and he was well aware of this lack, as was Rostnikov. At first Zelach, known to the investigators on the fourth floor as Zelach the Slouch, had been a pimple on the side of Rostnikov's small team, but gradually he learned that his survival was dependent on the good will of the inspector. When that realization came, Zelach discussed it at length with his mother, with whom he had lived his entire life. Zelach gave his loyalty to Rostnikov, though he never felt comfortable with his superior, never knew when the Washtub was making a joke or being serious, never knew when he might be making one of those jokes at the expense of Arkadi Zelach.

Karpo, as was usual in these meetings in the small questioning room, stood at near attention near the door, a notebook in his left hand, a Soviet ballpoint pen in the right. He stood behind Zelach, who had the constant urge to turn around and look at the gaunt detective to be sure that the sham of Zelach's life was not being penetrated by the emotionless, dark eyes.

"Zelach, you have that?"

Zelach nodded slightly with a wry smile of understanding, though he had no idea what he was responding to.

"At this point we have only the concern of a possibly disoriented parent," Rostnikov continued. "Since she came to us, we will make discreet inquiry and"—he tapped the neatly typed report in front of him—"I will begin to process your report for circulation to the proper agencies. That will take, I believe, about three days."

Karpo nodded almost imperceptibly. He had just been told by Rostnikov to put aside his current investigations and make inquiries into the allegations of Elena Vostoyavek that her son was planning to kidnap Commissar Andrei Morchov. Officially, he knew, they should report the incident immediately to the KGB. He also understood that Rostnikov planned to hold the report for three days so that Karpo could pursue the investigation. It was routine, but Karpo felt the necessity of recording his concern.

"I believe the ramifications of this incident make it essential that we inform the KGB immediately," Karpo said softly. At that moment Emil Karpo smelled lilacs and knew without putting words to it that he was receiving the first warnings, the aura of a migraine. The odors that came to him were always unbidden, evoking memories he could not quite identify from a childhood he preferred not to remember. Flowers, chicken zatzivi, cleaning fluid.

"And they will be informed," Rostnikov said. "By me, personally. This report will be in the hands of the KGB by this afternoon. I have the feeling, however, with their current range of interests it will take them a few days to give the situation their full attention."

Karpo nodded, took a note, and stood erect again. He knew that there were many ways to forward a report to another branch and be sure it was delayed or lost. The sender could present evidence of having forwarded the report, and the receiver would be embarrassed by its failure to follow through on the report. Karpo knew that Rostnikov had recently buried a sensitive report in the middle of a series of overly detailed accounts of forty minor cases of economic violations, ranging from the sale of fruit from an unauthorized stand on October 25th Street to the smuggling of two Canadian tires into Moscow in the van of a Leningrad Symphony cellist. As far as Karpo knew, the KGB had still not discovered the buried report.

"Sasha, you have the information on the missing bus," Rostnikov went on.

"Bus number forty-three on route seventy-five was reported missing at eleven forty-six this morning," Tkach said, looking up from his notebook, which lay open on the table in front of him. "The driver has a history of abuse of alcohol, and the assumption of the director of traffic for the sixth district is that he is asleep somewhere in the vehicle. I have issued a directive on the bus and driver to all uniformed and nonuniformed divisions. Other bus, taxi, and trolley drivers have been informed to look for bus forty-three."

"You believe he is drunk somewhere, Sasha?" Rostnikov asked, looking up from his notepad. "You know how many buses there are in Moscow?"

"There are four thousand, six hundred thirty-four buses in Moscow," replied Karpo, who resisted the urge to touch the left side of his head, where he knew the throbbing would soon begin. "This is the first time in the forty-six years of recordkeeping that a driver is reported to have taken a vehicle, though there are two reports, one in 1968 and another in 1975, of children attempting to drive away in city buses."

"You don't believe the driver took the bus," Rostnikov went on, looking down at his pad.

"I have drawn no conclusion," said Karpo. "There is insufficient information for a conclusion. There is only, at this point, history and precedent, both of which suggest that there may be another explanation."

"When an incident defies the statistics, what do we do with the incident?" Rostnikov asked, looking up.

Zelach turned uneasily in his chair. He was afraid the question had been directed at him.

"We incorporate the incident into the data base and

alter our statistics," replied Karpo. "There is no such thing as a transcendent or deviant incident or crime. All crimes must be part of the total if they are not to be lost."

Rostnikov nodded, and Sasha Tkach looked at his watch. If he got started on the investigation within the hour, checked to see if anyone had yet spotted the bus, perhaps he could wrap up before it got too late and be home in time to intercept his mother, who was going to have dinner with Sasha's aunt.

"So," Rostnikov went on, putting the final touches on his drawing of a coupling for a toilet pipeline, "do we have a theory or set of theories of criminal behavior that we apply to reported crimes, or do we gather information on the crimes and hope they tell us something, present a pattern, contain within them a direction or answer?"

Tkach shuffled in his seat. Rostnikov ignored him and waited for an answer.

"You wish me to acknowledge intuition," Karpo said evenly.

Rostnikov shrugged.

"I wish Tkach and Zelach to investigate the disappearance of a bus," replied Rostnikov. "I wish to know what they will do if no one reports having seen bus forty-three by the end of this day."

"It should not be difficult to find a bus," said Zelach, wanting to participate and thinking that he finally understood something that was being discussed. "A bus is . . . big."

"Perhaps we should get started," Tkach said, standing.

"The American detective Dashiell Hammett once had to find a stolen Ferris wheel," said Rostnikov. "He found it quickly, though no one reported a Ferris wheel parked on a side street or sitting atop a roof. How do you think he did this, Sasha?"

Tkach, who had taken a step toward the door, paused and ran his hand through his hair, brushing it back from his forehead.

"Why would anyone steal a Ferris wheel?" Tkach said impatiently.

"Precisely, Sasha. That was the question Hammett asked himself," said Rostnikov with a smile.

"To use its parts," said Zelach. "Or as a prank."

"Who would have the equipment to steal a Ferris wheel?" asked Rostnikov, pushing back from the small desk and reaching down to massage his leg back to life.

"The Ferris wheel was almost certainly stolen by a circus or a carnival," said Karpo. "They would have the equipment and a reason. They would also have the perfect place to hide it, in plain sight."

"Yes, Emil," said Rostnikov, rising. "And where might you find bus forty-three—if it has not been drunkenly absconded with by the driver? Zelach?"

"With other buses?"

Rostnikov nodded his approval.

"Who else has buses besides the bus company?" Rostnikov asked, this time looking down at the drawing.

"We will find out," said Tkach, putting his notebook in his pocket. Without another word, he was out the door. Zelach stood, paused for a beat to see if he would be asked another question, and, seeing that Rostnikov was occupied with his drawing, left the room behind Tkach.

"Emil," Rostnikov said as Karpo turned to the door, "do you know what meditation is?"

"There are," said Karpo, "a variety of definitions, ranging from engagement in concentrated thought on a specified and minimal subject to a relaxation technique that at its religious extreme strives for the absence of thought."

Rostnikov held up the drawing he had been working on. It looked to Karpo like a pair of rods connected by a bandage with a clamp on it.

"Each day is another layer of weight and complexity. If we are fortunate, we can keep from being crushed, but to do so we must have a portal to temporary peace, a meditation."

"Mystical," said Karpo.

"On the contrary, one of my meditations is plumbing," Rostnikov said. "Have you ever tried to get your building director to arrange for repairs? It can't be done. I do it myself. I do it with books and trial and error. I lose myself in leaks, plastic pipes, and wrenches, and when I am finished, in contrast to what happens frequently in an investigation, something that did not work, works. It is a meditation and satisfaction. If you have a leak, Emil Karpo, let me know."

"I would think your time could be better spent, Inspector."

"What is your meditation, Emil Karpo?"

"I neither have nor need one. I work."

"And you like your work," said Rostnikov.

"I am satisfied that within the parameters of our system and the reality of human fallibility I perform a worthwhile societal function," Karpo said.

"Do you know the story of the man who lost his ego?" asked Rostnikov, moving past Karpo to open the door. "It's Dostoyevski."

"No," replied Karpo.

"It is of no consequence. Let us go out and save Mother Russia from the criminals," Rostnikov said after a small smile. "And if possible, take care of ourselves at the same time."

Emil Karpo was not quite sure of what Rostnikov had just told him. The inspector had grown more and more cryptic and preoccupied in the past months. Karpo was sure it had something to do with Rostnikov's wife and son, Iosef, who, Karpo knew, was no longer in Afghanistan. Karpo also knew that Iosef was, or so Rostnikov had been told, on a special secret assignment for the army. Iosef was a pawn, a hostage of the state to keep in check the inspector, who had frequently stepped on the very large toes of the KGB. Though he had been much decorated and had nearly lost both his life and leg in the war against the Axis, Rostnikov had never, since Karpo had known him, displayed the slightest revolutionary zeal or interest in politics. And yet Rostnikov was known to be the most effective and relentless criminal investigator in Moscow. It was a constant puzzle for Karpo but one he tried not to address. To even consider it was a distraction from his duty.

As Karpo left the small office, Zelach and Tkach moved down the narrow aisle to the small head-to-head desks from which they worked.

"Where do we start?" he heard Zelach ask, though Zelach, officially, was the senior officer. "Wherever it is, let's stop for something to eat on the way."

Rostnikov emerged from the questioning room and moved slowly away toward the small cubicle that served as his office. The cubicle was a combination of plaster-board and plastic waist-high with windows reaching another two feet higher. There was no real door, just a narrow opening. Privacy was reserved for those of higher rank, which, several floors up, Rostnikov had once been. Porfiry Petrovich thought of none of this, nor of his wife or son, the plan he had for repairing the drain in the apartment of the Agarevas on the fourth floor of his building, or his leg.

He stood next to his desk, deciding that it would not be worth the trouble to sit down and then rise again. Rostnikov flipped the page of his notebook with the drawing of the pipe connection and looked down at the notes he had taken about Ivan Bulgarin, the man who walked like a bear. One of the notes was the phone number of the Lentaka Shoe Factory. Porfiry Petrovich picked up the phone on his desk and through the window of his cubicle watched Emil Karpo at his desk reach into his jacket pocket and pull out a plastic container from which he extracted a pill, which he put on his tongue and swallowed dry.

Rostnikov had noticed the signs of Karpo's headache, the slight rise of the left eyebrow, the dryness of the narrow lips, the almost imperceptible flaring of the gaunt man's nostrils.

Ten minutes later, after having talked to five people at the factory and taken three pages of additional notes, Porfiry Petrovich hung up the receiver and looked beyond his cubicle window through the windows of Petrovka and into an early-afternoon thundershower. Rostnikov hoped the winter would come early this year. He savored the blanket of white silence, the clean isolation of the cold. He picked up the phone again and dialed the five numbers that would connect him to the office of the Gray Wolfhound.

"It's raining again," Jalna Morchov said, looking out the window.

She had arrived home only minutes earlier in the bus provided for the children of people of influence. Their dacha was twenty miles outside of Moscow in one of the small villages unofficially reserved for "special" people, high-ranking party members, artists, generals, and KGB directors and department heads. The Morchovs' dacha was at the end of a lane protected by trees and a KGB car parked a few yards down the driveway. Jalna knew her father was home by the presence of the KGB car and the two men in it wearing brown suits.

Andrei Morchov, who had been busy preparing a massive report on production drops resulting from ethnic unrest in the Ukraine, had been spending less time at the dacha and more time in his Moscow apartment. Since Jalna's mother had died three years earlier, when Jalna was fourteen, her father had thrown himself into his work and into his mistress, a translator in the Telecommunications Division of the International Trade Center. Andrei Morchov was under the mistaken impression that his daughter knew nothing of Svetlana Petranskova.

Yuri had told her. Yuri had discovered the relationship in his weeks of following her father. Yuri knew a great deal about Andrei Morchov, who was putting on his coat as Jalna spoke.

"I must go back to the city," Morchov said, looking out the window past his daughter.

The Man Who Walked Like a Bear

Andrei Morchov was a man of moderate height and usually described as slender. His pale brown hair was receding from his forehead, but there was about him an aura of confidence, strength. Jalna believed that her father was not conventionally handsome but did have the power to mesmerize, and that power had kept him from going under through five regimes. Jalna believed that none of her looks came from her father. She liked to tell Yuri that she had inherited everything from her mother and nothing from her father. She imagined secretly that Andrei Morchov was not her father, that she was the result of a single night between her mother and some army private, though her mother had never given anyone reason to believe she was anything but the frightened wife of a determined and emotionless man. Jalna was and knew she was beautiful, that she looked like her mother, slender, blond, pale, wide of mouth, and able to draw the eye of any man.

"You will remain in the house for the rest of the day," her father announced as he buttoned his raincoat.

Jalna had no intention of remaining in the house.

"Yes," she said. "I have schoolwork to do."

"I will call to be sure you do," he said.

Jalna was sure he had no intention of calling, though he had been known to surprise her as he had surprised various enemies over the past three decades. It didn't matter. If he called and she was not there, she could claim later that she fell asleep or was in the bath. He might not believe her, but that, too, did not matter. What he wanted would make no difference by next week.

"Come," he ordered, picking up his briefcase. Jalna moved to her father and kissed his cheek as quickly and dryly as possible. Before she could move away, he grasped her arms and looked into her face. She returned the probing look.

"Yes?" she said.

"I see something in your eyes."

"What?"

It was probably a trick. He saw nothing in her eyes, nothing, she told herself.

"I don't know. My own reflection, perhaps."

He let her go and she stepped back, willing herself not to tremble.

"I haven't done anything," she said, trying to sound open, afraid her response might have a touch of defiance and a bit of telltale fear.

"And you'll not, not again," he said.

"Not that again," she said. "I'm going to my room."

"That again," he said firmly. "You'll never cause me embarrassment again. Never. That is understood. We do not discuss it. You know the consequences."

She opened her eyes wide, the practiced innocence of seventeen years. Their eyes met, and Jalna was determined to hold out, to meet him, to prove her unprovable innocence, but he, as always, held firm, his eyes unblinking until she turned away. Once, only once had she been with a boy before she met Yuri, and that was the one time her father had caught her, caught her in bed on a night he was supposed to be in Tbilisi for a conference. She had told Yuri two days after she met him at the American Club on Gorky Street. He had understood, but her father had not, never would.

"Be in bed by eleven," he said, moving to the door. "I don't know if I will be back before tomorrow."

The Man Who Walked Like a Bear

Jalna was tempted to speak, to say something acrid, but she held her tongue. There was no need or would soon be none. In a world of winners and losers, she had always been a loser and her father a *krepki khozyain*, a strong master. But things would soon change.

A smile swept her face, and her father touched her cheek as he moved past her and allowed a slight upturning of the right side of his mouth, which hinted at a smile.

As he went through the front doorway of the dacha and closed the door behind him, Jalna continued to smile, to smile at the picture in her mind of her father lying quite still and dead.

To get to the director of security at the Lentaka Shoe Factory, Porfiry Petrovich had to telephone the assistant to the factory director. The assistant, Raya Corspoyva, was the Communist Party representative at the factory. Rostnikov explained to her that he was conducting a routine update of the case of Ivan Bulgarin, who was now in the September 1947 Hospital. Bulgarin, he explained, had been involved in a minor incident at the hospital that had to be incorporated in his file.

Comrade Corspoyva said she understood and that it would not be necessary for the inspector to talk to the factory director. Instead, she told him what he already knew from the file.

"Comrade Bulgarin was an unfortunate victim of overwork," she said, and then paused.

Rostnikov, who was seated at his desk, fingered the pages of the American paperback novel on his desk and repeated, "Overwork."

"Yes," she went on. "Comrade Bulgarin was section foreman in plastic and leather processing. The factory is undergoing reform. Production was far behind reasonable quotas. The entire management had to be replaced." Another pause.

"I see," said Rostnikov. He was getting more information than he asked for, but he had no intention of stopping her.

"Comrade Bulgarin worked night and day," she continued. "He is a glowing example of a revolutionary zeal that has been all but lost. He is a party member, a dedicated citizen, one of the *peredoviki,* the model workers."

The woman sounded to Rostnikov as if she were reading a tract written in the 1930s.

"Almost a hero," Rostnikov said to break the latest pause. "How long did he work there?"

"Only a few months. He had been transferred from a wristwatch assembly plant in Kalinin. But he was magnificent. There was a slowdown in April. Comrade Bulgarin helped to break it. We need him back," she said. "Production and processing in leather and plastics have been down. There has been petty pilfering and—"

"Theft?" asked Rostnikov.

"A few tools, odd pieces of material. Minor, yes, but indicative of the morale crisis that must be overcome," she said emotionlessly. "You might wish to allude to that in your report, Comrade Inspector. Certain people might wish to consider further changes in the administration of this vital factory. Our nation cannot function without well-made shoes in which to work."

Rostnikov put the book in his pocket and followed the progress of a pair of uniformed MVD officers ushering a handcuffed man past Rostnikov's office. The man wore an open-collared shirt with a tie dangling from his neck. The man was thin, with a belly. The man was smiling as if he held a secret that would protect him.

"It would be awkward without shoes," Rostnikov admitted.

"You'll put all this in your report?"

"In detail," Rostnikov said. "Bulgarin had no family? No wife? No mother?"

"Correct," said Raya Corspoyva. "He was wedded to his work. Fifteen, sixteen hours of work each day. Six, seven days a week."

"A saint?" Rostnikov tried.

"A hero," she replied. "Saints are for the decadent."

Ten minutes after hanging up the receiver, Rostnikov was walking alongside Colonel Snitkonoy, who was on his way to the massive black Zil limousine with dark-tinted windows that would take him to a reception for visiting American businessmen. Normally the colonel strode through Petrovka and life with long steps, never looking to right or left. He moved slowly now, allowing Rostnikov to keep up with him, adopting the manner of a highly attentive superior listening to a sensitive report.

". . . a series of thefts at the Lentaka Shoe Factory," a clerk heard as she passed and received a nod from the Gray Wolfhound.

"And you wish to investigate personally?" the Wolfhound said conspiratorially.

"My staff is occupied with pressing matters that are fully documented in my day report, which will be on your desk when you return," said Rostnikov softly. "I believe I can deal with this quickly. Our nation cannot function without well-made shoes in which to work."

They stopped in front of the elevator, where the thin, smiling, handcuffed man with a belly was being attended by one of the two MVD officers.

"Boots," said the Wolfhound pensively. "Does the factory make boots?"

"I don't know," said Rostnikov. "But I'll find out."

"Good," said the Wolfhound, stepping into the elevator and facing front.

The MVD men entered the elevator with their prisoner and also faced forward. The thin, handcuffed man's eyes met Rostnikov's and the knowing smile suddenly disappeared, replaced by a look of panic. Rostnikov gave the man a small, wry smile and nodded almost imperceptibly. As the elevator doors closed, the man tried out a new smile, a slightly less mad smile of resignation.

Boris had driven the bus like a robot where he was told. The young man said turn, Boris turned. Right, left. It was hard to think of anything but the gun against his neck and the dead man who had been pushed down and out of sight by the man in the long coat. Boris was vaguely aware of passing the Yaroslavi Railway Station and heading away from the city on Rusakovskaya Street. A bus came toward him once and passed, and Boris thought the driver had a puzzled look on his face as he glanced at the out-of-route bus heading away from the city, but Boris had not looked closely. Perhaps it was only his imagination. Besides, did he really want to be discovered? What if the police did locate him, surround the bus? There would be shooting. What would the police care about the life of a loyal bus driver who had worked diligently for more than twenty-five years, who had never done anything to disgrace the company and had never missed a day of work for anything but illness and understandably bad reactions to vodka?

"Pay attention," the young man said. "We turn here."

Boris nodded. He couldn't speak. His eyes went up to the mirror. The older man sat about halfway back in the bus, looking out the window as if he were on his way home from work.

Perhaps it would be better if the police did come. These men might simply be planning to kill him when they got where they were going.

"What's your name?" the young man said. He was standing behind Boris and softly humming some foreign song.

"You already asked . . . Boris," the driver said, amazed that he could get sound through his dry lips. A small drink. That's all he needed. A very small one.

Boris drove the bus down a heavily rutted road in a broad field in which nothing seemed to be planted but miles of weeds.

"I . . . the road is too narrow," Boris chattered.

"It is wide enough," the older man in the back said softly, dreamily. "We measured. Drive slowly."

"Drive slowly," the young man repeated happily. "Are you excited, driver Boris? Afraid?"

"I have a large family, a wife, a mother, four children," Boris repeated his lie. If the young man had forgotten his name, he might also have forgotten their earlier conversation about the children.

"Too many children, Boris," the young man said. "Unpatriotic. You are not a good citizen."

"They are all adopted," Boris said. The barrel of the pistol clunked against his ear as the bus hit a wide dent in the road.

"Adopted?"

"Orphans," Boris said.

"You're a true hero of the revolution, Boris," the young man said. "And you are a liar. There, to the right, that house there."

Boris slowly turned the bus toward a small sagging wooden house in the open field. The road was even more narrow and difficult to navigate.

"You know what happens to heroes and saints, Boris?" the young man whispered. "If they are lucky, they become martyrs."

Chapter Five

Emil Karpo's head was aflame with pain. He ignored it. Or at least he worked through it. He was well aware that the pain was an impediment that even if ignored would take a toll, but he also knew that it would eventually—an hour, two or three at the most—pass. Perhaps the pill had had some effect.

He had purposely decided to walk in the hope that when he arrived at his destination the cool air would aid him and the pill would have time to work. He crossed Gorkovo to the City Hall side and moved south and downhill toward Red Square and came to a series of large, forty-year-old Victorian-looking apartment houses on the right.

He found the correct building and paused. In front of it, parked by special permit, was a black Zil, not unlike the one assigned to the Gray Wolfhound, but this one had gray curtains to hide the passengers from the gaze of the people on the street. The polished granite of the building that faced the street level in front of him came, Emil Karpo knew, from a quarry captured by the Soviet army at the end of the war against the Axis. The Nazis had planned to use the granite to erect a monument to celebrate the defeat of the Soviet Union. The building behind the granite facade and those surrounding it housed special people—bureaucrats, foreigners, including Americans and even Germans with business in Moscow, and upper-rank party members, *nachalstvo*, bosses like Andrei Morchov who also had dachas just outside the city.

There were far more prestigious addresses in Moscow: 26 Kutuzov Prospekt, for example, a nine-story apartment building where premiers, KGB chiefs, and ministers traditionally maintained vast apartments. The Gorkovo address was a bit safer, less ambitious, a statement that the inhabitants were content at their level, at least for the moment.

A well-built man in a dull, dark suit and striped tie looked at Karpo through the thick glass of the door. Karpo welcomed, savored the wave of sharp pain on the right side of his head followed by nausea. This wave had come before during his headaches. Mastering the unexpected was a challenge, a test that kept him on guard. That the challenge frequently came from his own body did not strike Emil Karpo as strange or ironic.

He opened his identification folder and displayed his photograph and identification card. The well-built man opened the door.

"Come," the man said when the door closed behind them.

The tiled entranceway smelled of lilacs, though Karpo

was sure that there were no lilacs nearby, that it was his migraine trying to trick him. He followed the man to a stairway in the rear of the building and they moved upward in soft light, wooden steps creaking beneath them. The man said nothing. Neither did Emil Karpo as they went up two flights and through a door that opened quietly onto a carpeted hallway. The man turned to his right and headed to the end of the hallway, where a door faced them. The man knocked gently, carefully, not too loud and insistent but loud enough to be heard if someone was expecting a caller. The door opened.

The slender man before Karpo wore a loose-fitting gray sweat suit. His hair was wet with perspiration and slightly unkempt. The man brushed his hair back, adjusted the glasses on his nose, looked at Karpo, and nodded at the man who had led the detective to the apartment.

Andrei Morchov nodded and the well-built man turned away and headed down the hallway. Morchov stepped back and allowed Karpo to enter. When the door closed behind them, Morchov produced a towel and dabbed his face as he led the detective down a small hallway decorated with Oriental figures and a metallic figure in bronze hanging from the ceiling.

They moved past a living room, also Orientally decorated, where a woman sat in a sweat suit that matched Morchov's. She was dark-haired, with a drink in one hand, a magazine on her lap. She looked up at Karpo, her face a mask, but Karpo sensed an inadvertent shudder as he passed. This time the wave of nausea was more brief. He controlled it easily.

The woman returned to her magazine as Morchov ushered Karpo into an office and closed the door. The office was not Oriental. It was stark, windowless, a single desk, a large desk with work neatly stacked upon it in bins. Two simple wooden chairs stood before the desk, and the desk chair itself was solid, wooden, unsingular. There were old file cabinets, and bookcases filled with worn books. The walls were empty except for a large photograph of Lenin looking to his right.

"You have four minutes," said Morchov, continuing to dry himself as he sat behind his desk and motioned to Karpo to take a seat across from him. Karpo sat and Morchov reached for a tumbler of slightly pink liquid. "I hope you don't mind if I don't offer you a drink. I have an engagement and will have to shower and dress for it very soon."

"I do not mind," said Karpo.

"My secretary said you have some information concerning a possible threat to my life," Morchov said, looking at the towel and placing it on the corner of his desk. "I find it difficult to imagine why anyone would want to kill me. It is an essential part of my political life that I do not always please those with whom I must deal. But it is equally essential for one in my position not to turn those with whom I disagree into enemies. The price I pay for this is that I have made no friends. I have betrayed no one, and there is no one who would consider me close enough to call my behavior betrayal even if we disagree."

"We have reason to believe that if such a threat is serious, it is, in fact, personal and not professional or political," said Karpo, hands folded on his lap.

"And," said Morchov after taking a drink, "do you propose to supply me with information concerning this possible threat?"

"At this point, we have very little beyond an overheard conversation by a woman named Elena Vostoyavek."

Morchov rolled his drink between his palms and continued to look at Karpo, who added, "The name is not familiar to you?"

"No."

"Yuri Vostoyavek: Is that name familiar to you?"

"No. Is he the one who has supposedly threatened my life?"

"Yes," said Karpo as Andrei Morchov finished his drink and placed the glass on the desk after wiping its bottom with the towel.

"Well, why are you wasting your time here?" Morchov said with a sigh. A knock at the door and Morchov said, "Yes?"

The beautiful woman with the dark hair opened the door. She now wore a white robe, and her hair was noticeably damp.

"We will be late," she said without looking at Karpo.

Morchov, unsmiling, held up his right hand and nodded. The woman left, closing the door gently.

"I do not wish to be late, Comrade," he said.

"I do not wish to keep you," replied Karpo.

"Who is this Yuri whatever?" Morchov said with an impatient sigh. "And why would he wish to harm me?"

"He is a young man who works as a messenger in the Central Telegraph Office," said Karpo.

"How young?"

"Nineteen."

"I will exercise some caution," Morchov said, standing. "There may be counterrevolutionary ethnic separatist groups that might wish to make a point. Terrorism is,

77

after all, not restricted to the Arabs. I doubt if this threat is serious, but I expect you to handle it quickly. Keep me informed through my assistant. I think there is no reason for us to speak again. You understand?"

Karpo rose and nodded.

"You may show yourself to the door," Morchov said. "Touch nothing on your way out."

Karpo left the room. The pain returned with an acrid surge, expanding within the left side of his head, ordering him to seek darkness, the quiet, enclosed tomb of his small room. When he left the apartment, the well-built man in the suit was standing outside the door expectantly, as if he had been called.

He nodded and Karpo followed him down the hall, wondering why Morchov had been unnecessarily rude.

When he got back to his small room, Karpo, in spite of the insistent pain that demanded that he capitulate, bow to it, checked the two sets of hair and the piece of dust he had pushed gently against the hinge of his door to be sure no one had entered. Emil Karpo turned on a small light and refused to close his eyes or even blink at the cold needles the light stabbed into his head. He would stay here in darkness for no more than half an hour. He would allow himself no more than that. He would then return to his duty even if he had to suffer through the searing pain, the almost unbearable light. But before he allowed himself the darkness, he picked up his phone, which he used only in pursuit of his duty, and called Porfiry Petrovich Rostnikov at Petrovka. The phone rang five times before the junior officer on duty picked it up and informed Karpo that Inspector Rostnikov had left word that he could be found at home going over reports. Karpo hung up and called Rostnikov at his home.

"I wish to report," Karpo said.

"Proceed," said Rostnikov.

And Karpo slowly, in detail, omitting only his own pain, related what had transpired in his visit to Andrei Morchov.

"I will have a full, written report on your desk this afternoon," Karpo concluded.

"Comrade Morchov sounds as if he may have some idea of why this young man might want to do him harm," said Rostnikov. "Or he may simply have a great deal on his mind, or he may simply be an unpleasant person. Who knows?"

"I was not antagonized by Comrade Morchov's behavior," Karpo said. "Though I did find it curious."

"Forget the report till tomorrow," Rostnikov said. "I won't get in till late in the morning. There are some thefts at the Lentaka Shoe Factory I must look into. I may need your assistance with this. Shall we have someone keep an eye on our young suspect? Yuri . . ."

"Vostoyavek," Karpo supplied.

"Get some rest, Emil Karpo," said Rostnikov. "You'll function better with some rest."

Rostnikov hung up, and Karpo did the same. Yes, Karpo knew he would function better with rest, and he would get that revitalizing rest by lying in bed fully clothed, but first he would change those clothes, wash, shave. During the conversation with Rostnikov, Emil Karpo had decided the pain would have to wait. He would not permit it to interfere with the performance of his duties. And, later, when he did lie down, he would leave the light on.

Emil Karpo looked around his room carefully before moving to the sink in the corner. His desk, shelves full of black notebooks on each and every case he worked on, the bed in the corner, the single wooden chair, and the squat, wooden dresser in the corner were in place, and the photograph of Lenin working at his desk was where it should be, over his bed.

———————

Porfiry Petrovich Rostnikov had just finished his right-handed curls with fifty-pound weights when Karpo had called. When he had come home an hour earlier, he had changed into his blue sweat suit, pulled the weights out of the lower cabinet in the corner of the living room, laid out his blanket, and arranged the wooden chair so that he was facing into the room with the music from the record player behind him. Recently, since Sarah's surgery, Rostnikov had found himself drawn to melancholy French music. He had traded six of his paperback American mysteries—two Lawrence Blocks, three Ed McBains, and a Jonathan Valin—for two very old Edith Piaf albums.

The weight routine required no thought. In fact, thought was to be avoided if at all possible. The workouts that left Porfiry Petrovich most satisfied, most refreshed, were those that passed without his being aware of time, passed with only a vague, blue-white hum instead of thought. But time had moved too slowly this night. He had sat on the chair, looked down at the neatly arranged weights, and smiled at his newest acquisition, a compact fifty-pound dumbbell from Bulgaria. It rested blue-black in front of him, inviting. He had listened to Edith Piaf sing about a piano and he had let the thoughts come, Sarah, the man who walked like a bear, his son Iosef, the Gray Wolfhound, Sasha Tkach's distracted look, Karpo's headache. The thoughts came and began to fade into the blue-white hum of soft music and the flow of energy and effort in his muscles.

The positions were awkward because of his leg, but Rostnikov had mastered them long ago. His lifts and repetitions were mostly for the upper body, arms, neck, abdomen, back. His good leg received a series of weighted rises near the end of the workout that ended with a painful but necessary manipulation of his left leg. When Sarah was home she usually helped him with the final manipulation. Rostnikov had been bending the leg and coming out of his blue-white peace when Karpo called.

Now Rostnikov put down the receiver and looked around the room. He would turn off the phonograph, put away the weights and blanket, place the chair back next to the table, and then shower, after which he would change, make the promised visit to his neighbors, the Agarevas, with his tools to fix the leaking pipe, and then return home to finish for the second time his Ed McBain novel as he ate his sandwich of black bread and thick-sliced cheese. He had one cucumber and four potatoes left plus a bottle of mineral water.

Rostnikov knew he would eat quickly, that the emptiness of the apartment without Sarah would be most evident at the table. He let the thoughts come back now, his wife and son, the people with whom and for whom he worked, but behind them loomed the large and melancholy shadow of Ivan Bulgarin, the man who walked like a bear.

———————

At the precise moment that Porfiry Petrovich Rostnikov was turning off his phonograph, Sasha Tkach was telling his wife and mother in great detail about his and Zelach's efforts to locate a missing bus and its driver.

"Put it on television," Lydia said, sipping her glass of tea. Lydia was small, loud, decisive, and inflexible. Unfortunately, she was, as even Maya had to admit, sometimes right. It was simply difficult to acknowledge that someone as maddening as Lydia Tkach could be right about anything. "Go on television and tell everyone to look for the bus."

"There are priorities," Sasha explained. "We would fill the television time with announcements of crimes. There would be nothing but descriptions of criminals, pictures of stolen automobiles, missing children."

The baby Pulcharia tugged at her father's pants and grunted. She was more than ten months old, crawling and good-natured. They were seated around the table finishing their Moscow-style borscht of beet soup, tomatoes, cabbage, and a bit of ham. Sasha reached down to pick the baby up and smiled at his wife. She returned the smile without enthusiasm. Missing buses were not what she wished to be talking about. She wished her husband to address their forthcoming move, to tell his mother that she would not be moving with them. She knew his pain, but it had to be done, and putting it off would not make the task easier.

"So," Lydia went on loudly, reaching over to pat her granddaughter's head, "so the television would be filled with crime. What is so terrible about that? It's better to see bald men reading the news and old men making speeches?"

"No one would watch," said Sasha.

"Nonsense," said Lydia. "They do in America. In America that's all they do now, show pictures of murderers and the people watch and go out and drag the killers in. What are they showing here on television that's better than murderers and bus thieves?"

Pulcharia leaned forward against her father and gave his neck a gentle, moist, and toothless bite.

"In any case," Sasha went on, "we did find one bus driver who says he saw the missing bus heading away from the city, far off its route, a short time after it was reported missing."

"Can we talk about something else?" Maya said softly, too softly for Lydia to hear.

"And no one else saw this?" Lydia asked, finishing her borscht. "Don't let the baby chew on you. It will make her sick."

Sasha sat the baby on his lap and whispered to her, "*Krasee'v/aya doch*," beautiful daughter.

"A man reported having seen an old couple get off the bus in front of the park," Sasha went on as the baby rubbed her eyes. "He didn't exactly report it. We followed the bus route and found him on a bench, an old man himself. He thinks he knows the old couple but we couldn't find them."

"Television," Lydia said. "You should put the baby to sleep. She's tired."

"Sasha," Maya said softly, taking the baby from his arms.

"Not tonight," he whispered back.

"What?" asked Lydia, reaching over to touch the baby.

"Sasha, she wants to know," said Maya.

"All right," he said with a deep sigh as Maya moved to the corner of the room to change the baby and get her ready for bed.

"What?" Lydia repeated.

"I . . . we," Sasha began. What remained of the evening, Sasha was sure, would not be pleasant.

Chapter Six

The uniformed man was standing at the window, looking across at a blank wall of stone. The wall, while not fascinating, did appear to hold his attention as the other man in the room gave his report. When the report was completed, the uniformed man spoke.

"Good. I want no mistakes, Vadim."

"No mistakes," Vadim said.

"The consequences of a mistake will be—"

"No mistakes," Vadim repeated. "We have him. As Lenin said, a single claw ensnared and the bird is lost. We have that claw ensnared."

The uniformed man at the window said nothing for perhaps half a minute and then turned and spoke.

"We have him when it is done. Understand that. And no one will be involved, have any specific knowledge but you, me, and Nikolai."

"I understand, Comrade," Vadim said.

The uniformed man now faced Vadim and looked into his eyes.

"The times are perilous," he said. "The romantics are taking over all across the Soviet Union. Weasels who cheered us yesterday, today call for rebellion, chaos, all in the name of freedom. Religion is no longer the opiate of the people. *Glasnost*, openness, an invitation to mindless mimicry of a decaying West, is worse than an opiate. Revolutionary goals have been abandoned. Soviet identity is endangered. You go down the street, turn on the radio, read a newspaper, and you'd think you were in New York or Rome. It cannot last. It cannot be allowed to continue. My father and his father lived, fought, died for the revolution. We cannot let it go to the god of Pepsi-Cola, Big MacDonald's, and Bruce Joels. We cannot have our history, our commitment demeaned by the triumph of materialism."

Vadim was attentive. Basically he agreed with his superior, though he thought the game they were playing was less philosophical and more pragmatic than the uniformed man had stated it. He was also uneasy about his superior's sharing of his thoughts about the project in which they were engaged. It was generally best simply to act and not to carry information that might later be an embarrassment, an embarrassment that his superior might decide to remove.

"Report again tomorrow," the uniformed man said abruptly, perhaps sensing that he had said too much. He moved to his desk and Vadim turned smartly and left the room. The corridors of the KGB building echoed with the clap of his shoes. It was late, but he still had work to do, things to check. There could be no mistake. His superior was certainly right. A mistake and they could both be facing something far more fearsome than the presence of the Pepsi-Cola Bottling Company.

Boris Trush rubbed the top of his head where he had just been hit with a stalk of celery. The stalk had exploded from the unexpected, at least to Boris, collision with his head, and pieces of vegetable had sprayed around the room.

"The man is dense," the young man said, looking back at the older man.

In the past few hours, Boris Trush had discovered the names of his captors. The older man was Peotor Kotsis, the younger his son Vasily. The other four people at the crumbling farmhouse had gone unnamed and, essentially, unseen since Boris had pulled the bus into the barn where he had been directed. Three men had climbed into the bus and had begun to move the body of the laborer as Vasily and Peotor had led Boris to the main house and the small room in which he now found himself nursing the emotional if not physical bruise of having been hit on the head with a stalk of celery.

"Look what I did," Vasily said.

Boris was seated on a bed in the corner.

"Look what I did," Vasily repeated, and Boris looked at the various pieces of celery he could see from where he sat. He also looked at the older man, who stood against the wall near the door, arms folded.

"Look what you made me do," Vasily amended. "You

are stubborn and stupid, Boris. I'm not trying to offend you here. Are you offended?"

"I'm not offended," said Boris.

"Good," said Vasily on his hands and knees, looking for a missing piece of stalk. "But you are stupid. You understand your situation here. If you weren't stupid, you'd be agreeing with me."

"But—" Boris said.

"No!" shouted Vasily, getting to his feet and throwing celery pieces on the table. "If you're not going to make sense, don't speak!"

"You wish to live, Boris," said the older man against the wall.

"Yes," said Boris.

"It wasn't a question," said Vasily with a sigh. "He was telling you. My father was telling you, reminding you."

"But we will be killed," Boris said in anguish.

Vasily removed his gun from his pocket and moved toward Boris on the bed.

"And what will happen if you don't?" he asked.

"This isn't right," Boris appealed to the elder Kotsis. "I'm just a bus driver."

"And that is precisely what we need," Peotor Kotsis said gently.

"You want me to drive all of you into Red Square so you can blow up Lenin's Tomb," Boris said. "We'll all be killed."

"Not necessarily, Boris," Peotor continued. "We do not wish to die, though we are willing to do so if necessary. We, Vasily, you, I, will all die eventually. This day, a year from now, ten years from now. There are causes bigger than ourselves, Boris."

"I'd like to choose my own causes," said Boris, cautiously keeping an eye on Vasily.

"But you do not have that luxury in this case," Peotor said. "You waited too long. Would you rather die with a bullet in your head here or die having changed history?"

"I don't want to make the choice," said Boris. "This is a nightmare."

"Life is a nightmare, Boris," Vasily whispered into his ear. "If you could enter my head for five minutes, you would know it."

"You have another ten seconds to think about it, Boris," Peotor said.

"No," Boris whimpered. "There are no bus routes near the square. You take the Metro or a trolley. We'll be stopped before we—"

"Eight seconds," said Peotor.

"You're not even looking at your watch!" Boris cried.

"Six seconds."

"I need a toilet!" Boris pleaded.

"Three seconds."

Vasily raised his pistol and aimed it at Boris's right eye.

"I'll do it!" Boris shouted.

Vasily put the gun at his side and said, "Welcome to our cause."

"He's just a man, a man at sunset," the apparently male voice shrieked from the phonograph.

Elena Vostoyavek looked at her son across the room and considered telling him, asking him to turn down the screaming man or woman, but Yuri seemed lost in thought, on a distant planet. He sat slouched in the worn sofa in the corner, the sofa Elena's husband had died on five years earlier. Yuri resembled him, was even sitting in the same position in which she had discovered Igor early that March morning. Elena wanted to tell Yuri that if he wouldn't turn the music down or off maybe he could move to a different position, unfold his hands, take that look from his face.

The man on the record shrieked more words about someone going to a meeting. Drums beat, horns blared.

"Come and eat before you go to work!" she called, waiting for something that resembled a lull in the sound her son thought was music.

"I'm not hungry," Yuri replied, closing his eyes as if any question she asked him, any comment she made, was a burden he could no longer bear.

Their apartment, two rooms, was in a block of 1960s ten-story white concrete squares near Vostochnaya Street. If an identical building did not block their view they would have been able to see the Palace of Culture of the Likhachev Auto Works.

"You'll be late," Elena said gently.

Yuri sighed deeply with the weight of the world upon him and stood up. He was, Elena tried to judge as objectively as possible, a handsome boy, blond, blue eyes, a bit slender, with a pouting mouth. She moved to his side to pull down his loose-fitting gray sweater, and he suffered her to do it for him.

"The music is loud, Yuri," she said gently.

"It is supposed to be," he whispered.

"But the neighbors . . ."

". . . think nothing of getting drunk, fighting all night," he went on, moving to the table to examine the bread his mother had put out. "If we are to hear every word of their banality through these walls of paper, then they can be entertained by my music. Besides, they've all left for work by now."

"Mrs. Gruchin is an old woman. She's . . ."

". . . almost deaf," Yuri said, moving to the record player as the singing man shouted as if warning him not to stop the concert, but Yuri did not heed. He pushed a button, and the noise ceased in midbeat. The arm of the phonograph rose and moved to the right, clicked off as the turntable stopped. And all was silence.

"He's louder than the American." Elena tried moving to the table to prepare him a thick slice of bread and a piece of cheese.

"The American is English," Yuri explained, moving to the table and accepting the bread and cheese. "He used to be a Beatle."

Elena worked at the Moyantka Carpet Store on the Arbat. She worked in the factory room and hardly ever saw customers, which suited her just fine. Elena and Vladimir Tsorkin cut remnants, trimmed rugs, kept the records, and supervised the cleaning and maintenance crews. Tsorkin was getting old and smelled musty like the old specials, the Oriental rugs in the locked room, but Elena liked him and looked forward to getting to work.

"I've got to leave, Yuri," she said. "I'll clean up when I come home. I'll get something special for dinner."

"I won't be home for dinner," he said between bites.

"Well, I would like to make you something special," she said, moving to the rack in the corner, where she retrieved her coat. "It's supposed to be cold and wet tonight. You could use the rest. You haven't . . ."

He looked up at her, pausing in midbite of a piece of cheese.

"What are you so nervous about?" he asked.

"Me? I'm not nervous. I just don't want you getting into . . . I don't know," she said.

Yuri shook his head, put down his bread, and moved to his mother at the door. He was about five inches taller than his mother and looked down at her.

"I worry about you, Yuri," she said. "You've been . . . thinking."

He smiled, put his arms around her, and kissed the top of her head.

"I'm sorry," he said softly, his head above her so she couldn't see his face. "I've had a great deal to think about."

"Don't do anything silly, Yuri," she said, pushing away from him and looking up into his face.

He grinned, the same grin he had grinned since he was a baby.

"I never do silly things, Mother," he said.

"I mean . . . the girl," Elena said. "You're going to see her tonight. That's why you won't be home."

Yuri didn't answer. He continued to smile down at her like a parent at an ignorant but much-loved child.

"Bring her here," Elena insisted.

Yuri shook his head no.

"Are you ashamed of me?"

Yuri shook his head no.

"She's not trying to get you to . . . do bad things, is she?"

"No," he said with a false laugh. "Where did you get such a crazy idea?"

"I'm late," she said, pulling her coat around her, checking her pocketbook, counting her change, fidgeting, unwilling to go through the door and leave him.

"I'll clean up and go to work, *Maht*. I'll be fine. No more music."

Elena smiled at him, a most unconvincing smile, and went out the door.

Yuri did as he said he would do. He put the bread, cheese, and tea away and cleaned the table with a damp rag. Then he washed his face, brushed his teeth with the last of the Czech tooth powder his mother had purchased almost a year ago, and combed his hair. He had much to do. He would go down to the phone in the People's Room of the housing complex and call Comrade Sukov-Helmst at the Telegraph Building. He would cough, speak hoarsely, say that he was going to the clinic with a terrible chill and temperature. Comrade Sukov-Helmst would be very understanding. Yuri Vostoyavek was not only a good worker who never missed a day, he was also Comrade Sukov-Helmst's favorite nephew.

Yuri moved to the phonograph, turned the screws holding it with his thumbnail, lifted the top of the turntable, and reached down to remove the small pistol wedged among the wires.

———

Lydia Tkach, much to her son's surprise, had not taken badly the news of her forthcoming expulsion from the household. At first, this had filled Sasha with relief. After she had changed the baby, Maya had left the apartment claiming that she had promised to visit Olga Stashak on the floor below.

Sasha had calmly, insistently told his mother of the decision, explained the difficulty of the situation, alluded to Maya's discomfort while insisting that the decision, the painful decision, was his. He had painted it as brightly as it could be painted, telling her that they would be nearby, that Lydia would be with someone her own age and with her own interests. Sasha had talked, waiting, expecting to be interrupted, but Lydia had said nothing. He was afraid he was speaking too softly, that with her poor hearing she had absorbed none of it, but when he paused to ask her if she understood, she nodded. And he had gone on, talking subsidies, visits, relatives, love, understanding, the cultural revolution, the history of Russia, the history of their family as far back as his memory would allow him to recall. Sasha, sure he had begun to sweat, had refrained from reaching up to push the hair from in front of his eyes.

And still Lydia had said nothing.

"What do you think?" he had concluded.

His mother had smiled knowingly, as if she had just received confirmation of some irony she had long suspected, but she said nothing, got up, took her teacup, and moved into her room.

For five minutes after she left the room, Sasha Tkach, who in the course of his career had shot a young man and several times almost been killed himself, who had confronted rapists, murderers, drug users, and religious and political fanatics, sat trembling.

The explosion from Lydia would come later. That was it. Lydia needed time to plan, to construct a response, a scenario. She would spring it on him late at night, the next morning, sometime when he didn't expect it. He would have to be prepared. But still he was grateful she had said nothing.

That was last night. Now it was morning, and the three of them sat at the table in silence, drinking tea, watching Pulcharia eat small pieces of boiled kasha with her fingers. Cups clinked, the baby babbled. Under the table, Maya touched Sasha's hand reassuringly.

Minutes earlier Sasha had received a call from Petrovka, a call he should be thinking about but could not.

Lydia finished her tea, rose from the table, pulled her black dress down to remove the wrinkles, and looked at her son.

"I have three words to say," Lydia said.

Pulcharia, startled, looked up at her grandmother and gurgled.

"Ingratitude," Lydia said. "Irresponsibility. Disrespect."

With that she strode across the room, grabbing her coat as she moved, and went through the door.

With the slam of the door, Pulcharia began to cry and Sasha Tkach realized that he had to rouse himself and go out in search of a missing bus and driver.

"I'm sorry," Maya said.

"I've got to go," Sasha answered, getting up.

"You did what had to be done," Maya said, taking the crying baby from her wooden high chair and kissing her cheek.

"She was right," Sasha said, moving to get his jacket from the closet. "I owe her a great deal."

"We all owe our parents a great deal," Maya said gently. "But we cannot spend our entire lives paying the debt. Parents should understand that. My parents understand that."

"You are missing the point," Sasha said with mounting irritation.

"And that is?" asked Maya, offering Pulcharia a bottle that the baby grabbed greedily.

"My mother should have time. She has no friends. She's alone. Damn. There's a stain on my jacket."

"Take it off," said Maya. "I'll clean it."

"No time," he snapped. "I'm late."

"I'm sorry you're so upset, Sashaska," Maya said.

Tkach hurried across the room and gave his wife and baby identical kisses on the cheek.

"You are blaming me, Sasha," Maya said as he opened the front door.

"I am not blaming you, Maya," he said with a sigh.

"And you are not kissing me," she said.

"I'm late," he answered.

"Then go."

And he went out the door, closing it hard behind him.

Zelach was waiting for him in a Zhiguli with a defective heater and the tendency to pull to the left. Tkach opened the passenger door and slid in.

"I've been waiting," Zelach said, pulling away from the curb.

Tkach grunted.

"I haven't had anything to eat," Zelach went on. "You know that stand at the Kiev Railway Station, the one where the Jews sell those meat pies?"

"Knishes," Tkach said with a grunt.

"Do you mind if I stop for a few?"

Tkach grunted and Zelach took that for an affirmation.

"Where will we start after we eat?" Zelach asked.

"They found a body," Tkach said, looking out the window. "Dumped on a road off the Outer Ring. Man named Tolvenavov. Shot."

"So?" Zelach said.

"He was due home last night," Tkach went on. "He takes route seventy-five; the missing bus was on that route. Computer put it together this morning after they fed in information from the dead man's wife. Made a match with our request for cross-checking on what we had about bus and driver. Shevlov called me when it came through."

Zelach nodded. Even copying machines were a source of confusion to him, a confusion he tried to hide with nods of understanding that sometimes got him in trouble.

"So, where do we go?"

"To the laboratory to see if the dead man can tell us something. Can I ask you something, Zelach?"

Zelach nodded uncertainly.

"Do you have a mother, Zelach?"

Zelach barely avoided hitting a grunting Volga that pulled ahead of him in a hurry as they moved off of the Borodino Bridge.

"Everyone has a mother," Zelach answered.

"She's alive?" Tkach asked, glancing at a young woman hurrying with a small suitcase toward the entrance of the Kiev Railway Station. He could not see the woman's face, but her legs were firm and long and he could imagine her heels clicking against the concrete. Zelach pulled over and parked the car, nodding at the uniformed policeman

Stuart M. Kaminsky

in front of the station who was about to order him on before recognizing the license plate and the driver.

"Yes," he said. "I live with my mother. You know that."

"I didn't remember," said Sasha.

"My mother has bad legs," said Zelach, opening the car door. "Can't walk much. You are lucky. Your mother is well, working, able to take care of herself."

"I'm very lucky," said Sasha.

"We're both lucky," Zelach amended. "You want a knish?"

"Why not?" said Sasha with a shrug.

Chapter Seven

Porfiry Petrovich Rostnikov listened as the factory manager gave him a tour of the Lentaka Shoe Factory. Raya Corspoyva, the party representative to whom Rostnikov had spoken the day before, accompanied them, a clipboard in hand, taking notes. The manager, a thin, balding, and very nervous man named Lukov, kept adjusting his frayed blue tie, which did not match his rumpled brown suit, though it did correspond with the manager's complexion. Lukov glanced constantly at Raya Corspoyva, a no-nonsense and rather good-looking heavy-set woman in a no-nonsense blue factory smock.

Lukov said something and pointed at a row of men and women at sewing machines. The machines were clacking so that the manager had to speak loudly to be heard. Rostnikov paid little attention. He was, in fact, enjoying the strong smell of leather faintly tinged with oil. He also enjoyed the row after row of partly finished shoes and boots of brown or black, shoes without soles, boots without heels.

"And up there, there in the assembly area," Lukov shouted, "we have a new machine for processing the leather by color, size, material! Of course, most of the shoes are not made of one hundred percent leather!"

"Fascinating," said Rostnikov, whose leg was beginning to warn him about prolonging the tour. "Can we go to your office and talk?"

"Of course," Lukov said expansively, opening his arms wide, showing that he had nothing to hide or fear, almost tripping over a mound of dark leather sheets the size of an open newspaper. Comrade Raya Corspoyva did not look pleased. She wrote herself a note on the paper attached to her clipboard. Lukov's mouth opened and his eyes moved to the clipboard in fear.

Minutes later the three of them were seated in a small office with large dirty windows looking out into the factory. The noise was muffled by the room but not completely obliterated, and the smell of tanned leather was replaced by stale tobacco. Lukov sat behind his battered desk, which was covered with a mess of papers of various colors. Raya Corspoyva sat at Rostnikov's side and straightened her already straight dark hair before placing the clipboard on her lap.

"Theft," said Rostnikov.

"Very little," said Lukov, looking at Raya Corspoyva for support. "Pilfering," he went on as she took another note. "Pieces of leather, even finished shoes. But even that is better since that television show. You know the one with Victor Shinkaretsky on *Good Evening, Moscow*."

"No," said Rostnikov.

The Man Who Walked Like a Bear

"He pretended to be a worker in a sausage factory," the woman explained. "Walked past guards who paid no attention with a gigantic ham hidden under his coat. Hidden television cameras got the whole thing. Factories all over the Soviet Union began a crackdown on security."

"But we had already begun. We had anticipated," Lukov added, leaning forward. "Would you like some tea, Comrade Inspector?"

Lukov's eyes were pleading with Rostnikov to refuse. Rostnikov said that he would not like tea.

"Ivan Bulgarin," Rostnikov said. The name made Lukov's mouth open and close like a fish.

"As I told you on the phone, Comrade," Raya Corspoyva said, "he is a fine manager. Overworked, in need of rest."

Lukov nodded in agreement.

"He said the devil was here," Rostnikov said flatly. "That the devil was trying to get him."

Lukov laughed, but when no one joined him, he stopped abruptly and reached into his pocket for a cigarette, which he lit nervously.

"The man is suffering from a temporary madness, Inspector," Raya Corspoyva said with a shake of the head.

"Of course," Rostnikov said with a nod. "But . . . when an accusation of theft is made, even by a madman, it should at least be investigated."

"You would be remiss in your duty if you did not," the woman agreed with a smile that conveyed an understanding of the breadth and difficulty of the policeman's job.

"Then," Rostnikov said, standing before the stiffness could begin, "I'll not trouble you further except for one question: Do you make boots in this factory?"

"Yes," said Lukov. "Fine boots."

The relief on the factory manager's face was childishly
evident as he crushed out his cigarette and rose. The
factory noise level rose suddenly behind them and Rostnikov
looked out as a small dirty-yellow lift truck with a pallet
full of boxes rambled into the center of the factory, seemed
to hesitate about which direction to go, and moved right
and tipped over, sending boxes crashing.

Rostnikov was fascinated but turned his eyes back to his
two hosts in time to see Lukov with a spaniel apologetic
look on his face in response to the woman with the clipboard, who made it clear with her tight lips and unblinking
stare that she blamed him for what they had just seen.

"Pardon me, Inspector," she said, hurrying to the door.
"I'm sure you can find your way out."

"Certainly," Rostnikov said and stepped aside. "Comrade
Lukov can show me to the door."

The woman opened the door, letting in the remaining
sounds of the factory. Most of the sewing machines had
stopped so the workers could watch the effects of the
accident, but those machines that needed no immediate
human direction continued to clatter. Raya Corspoyva
closed the door behind her and hurried, smock flying
behind her, toward the overturned lift truck and the driver,
who was being helped up by several co-workers.

"I'll show you out," Lukov said, trying to guide his
visitor away from the scene beyond the windows.

Rostnikov turned and followed the man to the door.
On the floor beyond the window, Raya Corspoyva looked
up at them as she stood over the driver of the lift truck.

"Handsome woman," Rostnikov said.

"I used to think so," Lukov said, leading the way through
the office door and into a dark corridor down which

Rostnikov had entered the man's office an hour earlier. "I mean, when you work with someone—"

"I understand," Rostnikov said sympathetically. "It is a great responsibility to run a factory like this."

"Great responsibility," Lukov repeated, opening another door and ushering Rostnikov through it and into a musty reception area past two women who looked up at them as they moved to the front door of the factory office. "We're told by people in the city what to pay the workers, what to charge for the shoes and boots, and they don't even know what our costs are. And we're supposed to keep the workers happy. How do you keep a worker happy? How do you produce a good product if it doesn't matter to anyone whether it's good or not?"

"It is difficult," Rostnikov agreed as they moved through the door and onto the concrete expanse in front of the factory.

"Let me tell you," Lukov whispered, though no one was in sight. "It's not just here. The workers don't care. Calls to produce out of patriotism don't work anymore. I don't think they ever did. Posters don't get leatherbound. I shouldn't be saying this, I know, but I trust you, Inspector. You have a kind face, an understanding face."

"Thank you," said Rostnikov, who was certain that Lukov, who was far from bright, probably took every opportunity to bare his soul to anyone when he was out of range of Raya Corspoyva.

"My father made shoes," Lukov said, looking around as if for a cab or a dead father. "My grandfather made shoes. I know leather. I know quality. You know where quality is? It's gone. I'm speaking treason here. My God. But we have a new openness, right? Gorbachev says so. Right?

107

Factories are allowed to make their own decisions, make a profit, give incentives, improve what they do. You know what it's like to spend a lifetime knowing you are creating an inferior product, knowing you can do better? What does that do to pride? I ask you."

Rostnikov shrugged.

"And so we have corruption and people who watch," he went on, nodding back at the factory to indicate that it held the woman who looked over his shoulder.

"Corruption?" asked Rostnikov. "You mean pilfering?"

"No," said Lukov.

"Corruption cannot exist without protection," said Rostnikov.

"Ha!" Lukov laughed until he coughed, which reminded him that he should fish into his pocket for a cigarette. "They get the best protection a ruble can buy. My God. I'm doing it again. I'm talking too much. It happens. I can't stop. My wife warned me. She wonders how I survived so long when I can't stop, but you understand, Inspector. I can see. This can't go on. Look there. That man. The one in blue. His name is Dovrinin. He's a colonel in the army. You know what he does? He sits there. All day. He sits there and he can reject any shoe, call it *brak*, junk, and he doesn't need a reason. If we are not . . . nice to him, he can reject everything, end our operation."

"That is no different than any factory," Rostnikov said. "Bulgarin, did he protest about some corruption?"

"Who knows?" Lukov lit his cigarette. "He wasn't here all that long, but maybe he found something, discovered something. A factory like this. Who knows where the money goes? If it loses enough, I get blamed and . . . I know what will happen. I know it. Someone will get caught, and they'll blame me. Millions of rubles. Do I see any of it? Does my family? No. I'll see the inside of a prison or worse."

He looked around and went on, "God, she may be watching us. She watches me all the time. I must be going as mad as Bulgarin."

"Bulgarin said the devil was after him," Rostnikov said.

"You said that before," Lukov said. "No more talk. My tongue should be torn out. Maybe it will be. All I want to do is make shoes. Smell me."

Rostnikov let his nose flare.

"I smell of leather," said Lukov with a sigh, looking at his cigarette as if it held some answer.

"Give me a name," Rostnikov said.

Lukov looked at the factory entrance in fear.

"A name," Rostnikov repeated softly. "You were waiting for someone to tell about the corruption of your factory. I'm listening. You may not get another chance. A name."

"There's nothing you can do," Lukov said. "I'll give you the name and then you'll have to forget it. Believe me. I told you. I feel better. I've got to get back to work."

"The name," Rostnikov repeated, almost whispering, his hand reassuringly on Lukov's bony shoulder, his head inches from the frightened man's face.

"Nahatchavanski," Lukov spat out. He pulled away from Rostnikov's grasp and ran back to the factory entrance where, indeed, Raya Corspoyva stood watching him.

Rostnikov had no car, no driver. He had come by the Metro and would head back that way. He had his Ed McBain book in his pocket but knew he would not read it. As much as we wanted to know what happened to the dead magician in the book, he knew he would open the book, stare at the page, and try to decide what he was going to do with the information that a high-ranking KGB member had just been accused of corruption.

———

Yuri Vostoyavek crossed quite illegally in the middle of Arbat Street, dodged a small black foreign car, and ignored the mad, angry honk of the horn behind him.

Yuri paused to glance at the newspaper that had been handed to him by a screaming man atop an overturned concrete flower planter in front of the Khudozhestvenny Cinema. He had seen the gathering of people when he came up from the Arbat Metro Station in Arbat Square and, though he was late, detoured to see what was going on.

The police, a group of brown-clad young men in brown hats, had arrived at almost the moment Yuri had taken the newspaper in his hand. The crowd had dispersed, moved suddenly away in a ripple while a young policeman ordered *ruki nazad*, put your hands behind your back. The screaming man being spoken to had resisted, but his arms were pulled firmly behind him by a trio of police, who ushered him away.

"Chaos," mumbled a well-dressed man with a briefcase who smelled of something sweet.

Yuri had grunted and watched.

"Freedom is not chaos," another well-dressed man had countered while they watched the police guide the screaming man with the armload of newspapers toward a parked car.

"It must be for the briefest moment or those let free

will not experience the light-headedness of realization and responsibility," a woman behind them said.

Yuri had turned to look at the woman, a small truck of a woman in a coat too warm for the weather and glasses so thick they made her eyes look like comic caricatures. She could have been any age.

"Stupid," said the first well-dressed man to Yuri.

"Engels is stupid," said the woman, turning to others in the small group of stragglers.

"You are stupid," said the second well-dressed man.

The woman, at that point, had swung a mesh shopping bag filled with oranges in a wondrous, almost slow-motion arc, striking the second well-dressed man directly in his face and seriously disrupting his confidence. The man staggered back against Yuri, who pushed him upright to face the advancing, squinting, relentless woman.

"Stupid," she hissed, and Yuri had turned away, though he would dearly have loved to see the outcome. In turning away, he ran into a man and with irritation looked up to tell the man that he should watch where he was standing, but the warning froze on Yuri's lips. He found himself facing a tall, gaunt, unsmiling man whose hands plunged into the deep pockets of his dark coat. His eyes met Yuri's and the young man felt that this pale stranger knew his every thought.

Yuri had moved around the man, may even have mumbled a *prastee't'e*, excuse me, and dashed across the square, behind a bus on Suvorov Boulevard, and then in front of the car on the Arbat.

He hurried down the Arbat. He knew, from his history in school, that the street was first mentioned in writings of the fifteenth century, but he was not interested in history now. He ignored the ancient houses, the little shops, and the large mansions on either side of the narrow, winding street. He paused for a moment in front of number 53, where Pushkin lived in 1831. Yuri neither knew nor cared about that part of the history of the street. He glanced at the newspaper in his hand and was momentarily surprised to see a cartoon of Lenin waking from a long sleep and looking around in confusion.

Yuri smiled at the sacrilege, folded the newspaper, hurried on, and entered a small church a block away. It wasn't crowded, but there were about fifty people gathered, listening to a priest who was in the middle of some mumbled ritual that Yuri neither understood nor cared to understand. There were no benches, no seats, and there was no way of simply characterizing the worshipers. Some were young—a couple with a baby—some old, men, and in the corner, looking toward him and the door, stood Jalna.

She smiled, a warm, somewhat pained smile that filled Yuri with love and longing. He moved forward, opened his mouth to apologize for being late, but she stopped him with a warm finger to his lips as the voice of the priest rose. The priest's eyes found Yuri for an instant and then moved on to someone else who had entered the small church. Yuri took Jalna's hand and stood silently, respectfully, but not listening.

Jalna's eyes were bright in the dim light of the church. She clutched his hand warmly and beamed. Yuri, infected, smiled with her and turned his head in the direction in which the priest had looked. In the darkened corner near the entrance stood a figure, a dark figure, a familiar figure. Yuri's grip tightened and Jalna looked at him, saw his turned head, and followed his gaze into the corner, where a man stood apart from the worshipers.

Coincidence, Yuri told himself. The gaunt man had been on his way here. He was no ghost. He was a coincidence, if, indeed, it was even the same man he had run into in the square.

Yuri fixed his eyes on the dark corner, unable to make out the face. He stared, determined to cause the man to back down. But the man did not move. The priest's voice rose and then dropped, indicating an end to the service or at least this part of it. The man in the corner did not appear to breathe. Yuri shuddered, and Jalna, sensing, feeling his fear, gripped his arm tightly.

Yuri turned toward her reassuringly as the crowd muttered a gruff, unfamiliar "amen." When he turned back to the ghost in the corner only seconds later, the man was gone.

"Yuri, are you all right?" Jalna said softly.

The couple with the child hurried to the door of the church and out into the cool air, neither looking to either side nor speaking to others. Worship was still a guilty pleasure. Anyone could be a KGB agent noting faces, taking names, gathering information for the moment when all this new freedom suddenly disappeared.

"I'm fine," Yuri said, leading her out the door. The ghost was nowhere in sight. "Are you hungry?"

Jalna nodded and they moved down the street to a *stolovya*, a small self-service luncheonette where they got in line behind a man in a workman's cap and scarf who hummed to himself.

Neither Yuri nor Jalna spoke till they had selected kvass and a bread pudding to share and sat in a corner away from the door, the other customers, and the humming workman.

"I heard him on the phone," Jalna said softly. She broke

off a small piece of the crisp pudding and put it in her mouth. Yuri adored the way she ate, talked. "He'll be sending me away in two weeks. He's told me nothing of it, nothing. He talks as if nothing is happening."

She would certainly cry now. Yuri was sure. He couldn't stand that.

"You won't go," he said.

"I can't do it," she said, looking around at the faces in the luncheonette, not seeing them. "I can't let you."

"If you go, I will never see you again. We will never see each other," he whispered, reaching for his kvass, knowing he couldn't drink it.

"You could join me," she said without expression, without hope or expectation. "We could defect. I don't care if I embarrass him."

"Jalna, there is no way I can get out of the country, get to Switzerland," he said with a sigh.

"We know what must be done, and it must be done soon, tonight, tomorrow," she said.

Yuri shuddered, remaining motionless for eternity, then shook his head yes. They had been through this before. There was nothing else to do if he and Jalna were to remain together, nothing to do but kill Andrei Morchov. He put his hand into his jacket pocket, came out with a small box, and handed it to Jalna, who slipped it into her purse.

———————

Emil Karpo had not gone into the luncheonette. He was sure, as he had planned, that Yuri Vostoyavek had seen and noticed him. The young man had reacted with guilt, apprehension. True, there were many things one could feel guilty about in the Soviet Union or anywhere else, but Yuri Vostoyavek had, upon seeing Karpo in the church, reached for his pocket as if to check that something was there or would be safe. Karpo, when he had been assigned early in his career to watching the large tourist hotels, had seen the same gesture by visiting businessmen who wanted to protect their wallets. It was a giveaway for the pickpockets, who would often bump into a mark in the lobby not to grab a wallet but to step away and see which pocket the mark would check. Emil Karpo had spent almost a year watching pickpockets, thieves, robbers, and their victims, and he had learned that almost anyone but a complete professional would react in giveaway patterns.

Yuri had given himself away, and Karpo had no doubt now that he had seen the young man with this girl that he was planning something and that whatever he was planning would involve something the young man was going to carry in his pocket. It wasn't there now, whatever it was, because Yuri had not actually touched the pocket and there was no bulge in the pocket beyond a few coins that Karpo had heard jangling as the young man walked.

He could see them clearly, though they could not see him. He stood across the street behind the window of a furniture shop. The woman who ran the shop had risen to take care of him when he walked in, but Karpo had simply looked at her unsmilingly and turned to watch the couple through the window. The woman who ran the shop had smiled falsely as if she did not care and had returned to her seat behind a counter to hope for the early departure of this less than welcome intruder.

Karpo watched the unheard conversation of the two young people. If they were conspirators, they were not happy ones. Their faces were pale with dread, resignation. At least that was clear in the face of the young man. The girl's face, beautiful, bright, unmarked, and clean, was more difficult to read. It was also clear that they had come to a decision. The young man said something, looked around to be sure no one was listening, watching, and then leaned back in his chair as if something had ended. The girl had stopped eating, turned to look at the young man with concern, and touched his cheek reassuringly.

Karpo shuddered with recognition from a depth he did not understand. He could almost feel the touch of the hand on his cheek, smell the girl. He also knew that in the aftermath of a migraine he could count on a weakness in the knees for a good part of the next day and an inexplicable connection, a needle-thin connection to elusive memories of the past. Karpo tried to catch the memory of the hand against his cheek and then dismissed it, ordered it away with an anger that must have showed on his face, for behind him the woman who owned the shop said in a quivering voice,

"Can I help you, Comrade?"

"No," Karpo responded, watching Jalna and Yuri finish their snack and head for the luncheonette door.

Emil Karpo knew without thinking or acknowledging that he was one week and two days from his next meeting with Mathilde Verson, the prostitute with whom he met, coupled, and relieved himself once every two weeks. Perhaps it was the touch of Mathilde's hand against his cheek that he remembered, but he could recall no waking moment in their relationship when she had attempted to touch him tenderly, when he had permitted her to do so. And she had understood, understood that a barrier existed through which their relationship could not pass if Emil Karpo was to retain his identity. A break in that identity, that persona, might be devastating. Mathilde had respected that barrier, had treated him with a tender amusement.

Emil Karpo was sure that he did not need her specifically, that he exercised only animal needs, needs he accepted as a limitation of the human species, and yet there were moments when Mathilde ... The young girl and Yuri Vostoyavek walked onto the Arbat and looked around, seeing small crowds, people passing, and moved to their left, heading again toward Arbat Square.

Without looking back at the woman in the shop, Karpo stepped into the street half a block behind the couple and followed them at a safe distance. He repressed the feelings he had. When the aftermath of the migraine was gone in a few hours, it would be no problem. Then he could think and not feel. Emil Karpo was a police inspector. He had his duty, and his duty was clear, as clear as the law. If others evaded the law, moved around it, teased its corners, corrupted it, it would not deter him from his duty. Compassion would lead to destruction. The law was all there was, the law and the State, which created the law. There was no morality, only law. He thought it, almost said it to himself, but deep within him a vague face he could not identify was smiling.

———————

The man in the suit stood for only a few moments at his

window in the KGB's building at Lubyanka. He had spent an uneventful evening and night with his wife and a cousin from Kiev who was in Moscow for a trade union assembly. The cousin had suggested, when the children were not present, that the effects of the Chernobyl disaster were still being felt, that fruit was checked in the Kiev markets, that the nuclear power generators were actually back on but that workers remained only two weeks before being rotated.

"The radiation levels are beyond the minimum even two hundred miles away, but they're letting old people return," the cousin had whispered.

"They shrug and say, 'What difference does it make?' It takes twenty years for the radiation to kill them and they'll be gone from something else long before that, but they'll outlive their dogs."

The KGB man had said nothing, nodded, leaving the conversation to his wife, thinking about other things.

"And," the cousin went on softly, leaning across the table as if bugs were planted in the walls, which the KGB man knew was not the case because he checked at least twice each month, "and, the reports are coming in from Yugoslavia. People are dying of cancer. Statistics are far beyond the normal. They won't be able to keep it under wraps for long, I tell you. I'm doing what I can to get Yana and the children out. That's why I'm here for the trade union meeting. I was hoping . . ." He paused.

The KGB man knew what was coming. He looked up from his thoughts into the eyes of his cousin and waited.

"I was hoping you might use . . . some influence to get us, the children, me transferred," the cousin said, a trail of sweat on his brow from the extra glass of cognac he had needed to gain the courage to make the request.

The KGB man's wife kept her head down and ate as if she had heard nothing. The cousin's wife bit her lower lip.

"I have no influence with the trade unions," the KGB man said evenly.

"Well, not directly," said the cousin with a small laugh. "Of course not. Not directly. I know that, but if you wanted to—"

"I'll see," the KGB man said.

"It's not as if—" the cousin's wife said, her voice a tremulo.

"I'll see," the KGB man repeated, making it clear that the conversation was over.

They had finished their drinks with small talk from the KGB man's wife about the availability of Siberian fruit. The evening had been interminable, but the children had remained quiet and distant, obviously having been told that important things were going on and their father's cousin should not be disturbed in any way.

And now the KGB man stood in his office, the only place where he felt at peace, and considered whether he would help his cousin. It might be a good idea and it would cost him little beyond a phone call. Then the cousin, who was a ranking member of his trade union, the district power and utilities union, would owe him more than a favor. He would owe him a great debt and possibly be in position to repay it in the future. But that was the future. He moved to his phone, lifted the receiver, pressed a series of buttons, and gave his rank and name to Vadim, who had reported to him the day before.

"It proceeds," Vadim said.

"Good."

"He is going ahead with the investigation as we planned," Vadim reported.

"Keep him interested," the KGB man went on.

Both men knew well enough not to give details, names over the phone. Later, if questioned about the conversation, they had another case they could claim to be the subject. If it came to that, however, there would probably be no opportunity for further deception.

"Report as you get additional information," the KGB man said, and hung up the receiver.

There was other work to be done. He moved to the desk, arranged the reports in front of him, and reached for his pen and a white pad of paper. He removed the glasses from his pocket and put them on his nose and around his ears. There was a computer in the room, but anyone could gain access to what he put on the computer. Someone could be sitting in another room of the vast building reading his words, his numbers, even as he considered them on the screen. No, he had learned long ago to put everything on paper first, work out what he could share and was willing to share. His own notes he shredded and each night he took the shreds home to burn even when the notes were innocent.

A bad habit could destroy a man.

As he wrote, he wondered where the policeman was at the moment. If a smile were within him, he would have smiled now, imagining the puppet going through the motions the KGB man was dictating.

Chapter Eight

The hospital administrator looked nervous, a nervousness he attempted to hide behind a mask of bureaucratic overwork.

"Transfers," said Schroeder with a sigh, brushing back his hair, pulling down the lapels on his jacket, adjusting his tie and glasses. "Do you know how many transfers we get in a week? Six, seven. The forms, paperwork. It doesn't end. My father wanted me to be a career soldier. Perhaps I should have listened to him."

"Perhaps," Rostnikov agreed.

They were standing in the record room down the corridor from Schroeder's office. Two people worked in the room, which held dozens of file cabinets and a single computer in the corner. The two people, a man and a woman, did their best not to pay attention to the new administrator and the box of a man who walked with a limp.

"It was his family's idea," Schroeder said, going through the files furiously and then turning to face the detective. "Not here. It was only yesterday. They get a copy. We keep a copy. It's probably still somewhere. It's not my fault. In the few months I've been here, the bookkeeping system has improved two hundredfold, but there's still so much . . . the papers could be anywhere."

The man's arms went up to indicate that, indeed, anywhere meant anywhere in the universe.

"But it will turn up. It should be on my desk. It will be on my desk."

"Ivan Bulgarin was transferred to another facility at the request of his family," Rostnikov said evenly.

"That's what I said," Schroeder said, looking at the two records clerks, who seemed to be absorbed completely in their work.

"And you don't remember where he was transferred?"

"It's in the records if I can just—"

"Who would remember?" Rostnikov went on. "A nurse, doctor?"

"I'll ask," said Schroeder. "I wasn't here, you remember. And the night nurse doesn't—"

"Let's ask," said Rostnikov gently.

"It wouldn't do—"

"Let's try," Rostnikov insisted gently.

Schroeder was trapped.

"Well, if you—"

"I do," said Rostnikov, touching Schroeder's shoulder.

And they went in search of someone who might be able to tell them what had become of Ivan Bulgarin, the man who walked like a bear.

The Man Who Walked Like a Bear

Boris Trush nodded his head in complete understanding of everything that was being told to him. He nodded his head and began to make a plan.

"We will drive slowly past the Alexander Gardens," Peotor Kotsis explained as they walked through the dried-out field behind the wooden house and barn where Boris's bus was parked. Boris had been given a torn pair of cloth pants and a rough sweater so his uniform could be kept neat and clean for the big day.

"Past the Alexander Gardens," Boris repeated.

Peotor Kotsis had long since removed his coat and now wore a pair of blue pants, a white shirt, and a sweater. The madman looked like a distinguished professor with dark hair and scholarly gray sideburns. But there was no doubt the man was mad, not as mad as his killer son, but quite mad nonetheless.

"Across Fiftieth Anniversary of the October Revolution Square behind the State History Museum," Kotsis went on.

"Behind the State History Museum," Boris parroted. Across the field, Vasily, his weapon slung over his back, was talking earnestly to three young men and a young Oriental-looking woman. Vasily seemed to be upset with them. Boris did not want Vasily upset with him. It took very little to upset Vasily, and the result of upsetting Vasily could be fatal.

"Then," Peotor went on, "past Twenty-fifth of October Street in front of the State Universal Stores." He paused as they walked.

"Past GUM," Boris acknowledged.

Across the field, Vasily laughed and began kissing each of the young people in turn, ending with the young woman, who got an especially long kiss.

"And then into the square," Peotor said. "We move slowly, a busful of visitors, lost, cameras in hand, past the marble stands by the Senate Tower, right up to the Lenin Mausoleum. When the guards move forward to stop us, we will rush out of the doors of the bus, we will eliminate them, destroy the tomb, and be gone before they can react. We'll all go in different directions. The crowds will be wild. Confusion. They've never faced a real threat. They won't know what happened till we call the foreign press and tell them. You'll get lost in the crowd, too, Boris. Lost with our gratitude. I'm sure you won't give us away."

"I won't," said Boris earnestly. "You have my promise."

The lie was evident. Boris knew that they would kill him the moment he got them to the tomb. They couldn't let him get away.

Peotor suddenly stopped.

"My people have asked to be heard for almost a thousand years," Peotor said, looking south in the direction of the province from which he had come. "We have not been allowed to speak until now. Now voices are being raised throughout the land and we are allowed to speak, but Boris, the irony is that no one will listen. Georgians, Armenians, even Mongol mongrels are being heard, but we are considered to be too small and too weak. The world will notice us after this, Boris Trush. The world will notice and we will be part of history."

"They'll hate you," Boris said, knowing he had no chance of prevailing.

"Yes," said Peotor. "At first they will. There will be days, weeks of shock, but our cause will be explored in magazines, newspapers all over the world. We will no longer be ignored. We must be heard, Boris. We must be heard or the lives of our fathers and mothers and theirs before them for a dozen generations will be meaningless. Do you understand?"

"Perfectly," said Boris. You are insane, Boris thought. That is what I understand. You are insane. I need a drink and I have to hope I have enough nerve to do what I must to save my life.

Vasily was now trotting across the field toward them with a smile on his face. The gun strapped around the young man's back jostled. Thunder cracked in the distance, and Boris hoped that he would neither step back nor cringe when the young and smiling lunatic came upon him.

———

"You know what this is?"

Kostnitsov spoke as if he were addressing a severely retarded child. Kostnitsov was somewhere in his fifties, of medium height, with a little belly, straight white hair, poorly cared for teeth, and a red face more the result of his Georgian heritage than his intake of alcohol, which was moderate. He was an assistant director of the MVD laboratory but he had little or no contact with the director and had no one working under him. Kostnitsov wanted no assistants, and it was clear to everyone that none would be able to tolerate him. Boris Kostnitsov was left alone in his unnumbered laboratory two levels below the ground in Petrovka.

Now, standing in his lab and wearing a blue laboratory coat and a scowl, he held out his hand to display to the two policemen something formless and quite bloody.

Zelach looked at Sasha Tkach for an answer, but Sasha's thoughts were elsewhere.

"A heart?" Zelach guessed.

Kostnitsov looked disgusted.

"A heart? This little thing looks like a heart to you? Does your little finger look like your penis? In your case, possibly. A penguin has a heart this size, not a human. Tkach, what do you say?"

Kostnitsov held the bloody blob under Sasha Tkach's nose. Tkach looked down at it emotionlessly.

"A liver," he guessed.

"A liver," Kostnitsov repeated incredulously. "This bright-red organ looks like a liver to you? This is a human organ. A human liver is dark, firm, unless, of course, it is diseased."

Kostnitsov began to pace between his cluttered laboratory tables and his even more cluttered desk, which held, somewhere beneath the books and papers, a bottle in which it was rumored Josef Stalin's spleen resided.

Zelach looked at the desk and blurted out, "Spleen."

Kostnitsov stopped pacing, dropped the slithery organ in a metal bowl, placed the bowl on the lab table, and turned to Zelach with a grin.

"There's hope for you," he said, advancing to Zelach and patting him on the cheek with a still-bloody hand. Zelach stepped back and looked around frantically for something reasonably clean with which to wipe his face. Seeing nothing he would be willing to use, Zelach moved to the sink, turned on the water, and washed, while Kostnitsov turned his attention to Tkach.

"The spleen," Kostnitsov explained as if to an avid student, which Tkach was not, "is one of the largest lymphoid structures, a visceral organ composed of a white pulp of lympathic nodules and tissue and a red pulp of venous sinusoids in a framework of fibrous partitions lying on the left side below the diaphragm, functioning as a blood filter and to store blood. It is said to be either the seat of melancholy or mirth. An underappreciated and quite poetic organ."

"Quite poetic," Tkach agreed.

"The bullet went through the heart," Kostnitsov said, weaving his bloody hand as if following the trajectory of the missile through an imaginary body. "It moved down through the left lung and heart, shattering a rib, and ending its journey in the spleen. Remarkably little damage to the spleen, but man cannot live on a spleen alone. Are you listening, Comrade Tkach, or am I boring you? Are your thoughts of university girls on the grassy Lenin Hills?"

"I'm listening," said Tkach, who stood, arms folded, as Kostnitsov pushed his face forward in front of the detective.

"You want to know about the bullet? What?"

"I want to know whatever you know that could help us find who shot Tolvenovov," said Tkach. Zelach had finished washing his face and was drying his hands on his rumpled trousers.

"You want some tea, coffee?" Kostnitsov asked.

"Information, opinion," said Tkach, who knew, as did every other MVD investigator and uniformed police officer, that Kostnitsov was probably a bit mad, certainly offensive, and possibly the best forensic scientist in the Soviet Union.

"Information. You have the man's name, the make of

the weapon that killed him," said Kostnitsov, moving to his desk, pushing away some papers, and picking up a cup of tepid liquid, which he put to his lips. There was a bright glow in the scientist's eyes as he looked at the two detectives.

"The victim was about to struggle when he was shot," Kostnitsov said. "His right hand was still in a fist, and judging from the calluses on his hands, he was right-handed. From the path of the bullet, it is clear that he was just rising from a sitting position when the bullet struck. The shot surprised him. He didn't turn away."

"Go on," said Tkach when Kostnitsov paused and looked at Zelach, who was standing near the door, as far from the scientist as he could get.

"The man was shot on a bus," said Kostnitsov.

Tkach was suddenly quite alert.

"How . . . ?"

Kostnitsov opened his mouth and pointed to his teeth before he spoke.

"When he died he pitched forward, hitting his teeth on chrome. I have a small piece of chrome I took from his tooth. The report said this might have something to do with a stolen bus, so I got a sliver of chrome from a bus seat this morning. Same. But more. Our victim slumped or was pushed down after he was shot, and the open wound in his chest scraped along the bus seat picking up bits of plastic, inferior quality. That, too, I checked by getting a sample from a bus this morning."

Kostnitsov paused and looked at both detectives, waiting.

"Karpo should have this case," Kostnitsov finally said when he had no response, no applause. He finished his drink and put the cup down on a pile of precariously balanced books and papers. "He knows how to appreciate professionalism."

"Your conclusions are remarkable and quite helpful, Comrade," said Tkach.

"I know that. I know that. I know that. You know how small the particles are that I had to work with? And do I have decent equipment?"

He looked around the laboratory, as did the two policemen.

"I wouldn't know," said Tkach.

"No," said Kostnitsov. "I do not. Can you imagine the miracles I could perform with an electron microscope? Not that I can't do almost impossible things now."

"Can you tell me who killed the man on the bus?" Tkach asked.

"Yes," said Kostnitsov with a grin, showing most of his ill-treated teeth.

"Then make our jobs easy. Give us his or her name and we'll get a nice commendation from the party secretary," said Tkach.

"The person who pushed the victim down may not have fired the gun," said Kostnitsov. "The person who pushed him down was about forty-eight years old, a man, probably medium build, white and pale, dark hair with a bit of gray in it. If you find a suspect I will give you a definite identification."

Zelach, in spite of himself, laughed, then wished he had not. Kostnitsov advanced on him.

"DNA," hissed the blue-smocked wraith in Zelach's face. "Do you know what that is? It is in every cell of your less than adequate body. You identify a spleen and don't know what DNA is. Is there hope for such an unbalanced creature?"

The medicinal smell of the lab was beginning to make Tkach ill, that and the memory of a recent knish. He had a sudden internal flash of Kostnitsov opening his stomach and examining the contents, including the knish, to determine the precise moment of his death. Tkach wanted to flee.

"DNA is the genetic material," Tkach said.

Kostnitsov nodded and turned to him.

"Each person has his own pattern," the scientist said, moving to his desk, pushing papers away in search of something as he spoke. "It is better than fingerprints. The odds of duplication are almost nonexistent. Every cell in the body has this print. Our dead man grasped the wrist of the man he was about to strike. He picked up a few surface cells and even a trace of hair. You bring me even a strand of hair of this man and get me into an electron microscopy laboratory and I will identify him."

"Amazing," said Tkach, which was just what the scientist wanted to hear. Kostnitsov found what he was looking for on his desk, a pad with notes and numbers scratched on it. He brought the pad to Tkach, who asked, "Can you tell us anything else?"

"Other people handled the body," Kostnitsov said, pointing to the pad in front of Tkach's hand. "One of them was a woman. All of them except the first man are young, relatively young, younger even than you. At least three of them, including the first man, were Turkistani."

"Turkistani?" Zelach asked before he could stop himself.

"Conjecture, conclusion, but almost certain," Kostnitsov said, still taking his pad back from Tkach. "Tobacco bits on the victim. Someone who carried him. Turkistani tobacco. Also one small thread of a jacket made with wool dyed in Turkistan. Wool not sold in Moscow. No one would want it if it were. Inferior material. But who knows what people will wear?"

"You are sure?" said Tkach.

"No, I am not sure, but the weapon is one that has been linked in reports—number ten twenty-three, January last year; number four thirty-two—eleven, Kirov, April this year; four others all linking the Stechkin with clashes involving Turkistani separatists. Look at the computer. Madmen and madwomen."

Zelach couldn't imagine anyone nearly as mad as Kostnitsov but he said and did nothing to betray his thoughts.

"We are looking for a medium-height Turkistani about forty-eight years old," said Tkach.

Kostnitsov nodded and looked at his pad.

"Do you read poetry, Comrade Inspector?" the scientist asked.

"Occasionally," Tkach said, which was true primarily because Maya thought it was romantic to be read poetry to late at night. If the conditions were right and Lydia were not snoring too loudly in the other room, and the baby wasn't restless, Maya would . . .

"Good," said Kostnitsov. "Because facts are of no use without poetry. It is poetry that makes sense of facts. You understand. Get me an electron microscope and I'll make real poetry. I'll see into the very soul of a chromosome, the secret segment of a twisted thread of the very fabric of human existence. I'll imagine myself into the smallest piece of evidence and give you the very face of criminal and victim. Is that not poetry?"

"It is poetry," Tkach agreed.

"I have work," Kostnitsov said with a sigh, turning away from the policemen. "Next time send Karpo."

The scientist moved to a white metallic box on his lab table. The box was marked in ink with the words "Clopniki Investigation—Foot."

Zelach and Tkach departed before the box was open.

———————

There is a point, Rostnikov knew, at which you must stop pushing or the balloon will break. When he was a small child, he had heard about balloons, thought they were the most amazing things imaginable, wanted desperately to see, touch one. Finally, one morning when he was no more than five or six, he was walking to the market on Herzen Street with his mother and saw a man with balloons, white balloons. There were slogans written on the balloons, and children were flocking around the man. There was no helium, no gas of any kind in the balloons, but they jostled upward and back in the wind.

Porfiry Petrovich's mother had watched her son turn his head to the balloon man as they passed, and though they were late and the lines would be so long at the market that they would have to wait many hours for whatever food, if any, was available, she let him stop, let him join the other children.

Porfiry Petrovich had reached over the shoulder of a little girl to touch a single, stray balloon that dipped toward him. He had stretched, strained, and finally, when the balloon fluttered down over the heads of the screaming children, Porfiry Petrovich and the little girl had both touched the balloon. The little girl had grabbed the sphere and smiled at Porfiry, and the two of them had explored the soft, strange thing while the balloon man chatted, encouraged the other children, and held the balloons aloft out of their reach.

And as Porfiry and the little girl touched the balloon that they held between them like a magical bubble, it burst. Porfiry was never sure whether it was his touch or hers that broke it. The moment of ecstasy was replaced by fear. Porfiry had looked around for his mother. She was hidden by the crowd of children who had turned to him and the little girl with the deafening pop of the balloon.

The tall balloon man had stepped through the crowd and looked down at Porfiry, who stood close to the little girl. She had taken his hand. The man leaned down to Porfiry and the girl. Porfiry could smell his breath, the dry, distant odor of tobacco like his uncle Sergei.

"What is your name?" the man had said.

Porfiry held back the tears, eyes darting for his mother, hand holding tight to the little girl's fingers.

"Porfiry Petrovich," he had answered. He could not remember if the little girl had given her name.

"Remember this, Porfiry Petrovich," the man whispered in his ear, raising his eyebrows to play to the crowd of children, who laughed. "Treat precious things gently. If you press the balloon too hard, it will break. Will you remember that?"

"I will remember," Porfiry had said.

"Good!" the man had shouted, standing up. "Then here is a gift."

He handed Porfiry and the little girl each a balloon

on a string and turned to the crowd of children who clamored around him, begging, calling, crying for a balloon of their own.

The little girl had dropped his hand and run away, and Porfiry Petrovich had raced around the crowd and found his mother.

"What is written on the balloon?" he asked.

"Sacrifice for the Revolution," she said. "There's a free circus tonight. That is the theme."

The balloon had lasted almost till evening before a small leak drained and withered it.

"Porfiry," Sarah said gently.

"Yes," he answered, looking at his wife in the bed. The sun was going down and the ward lights would soon be coming on, the harsh white lights that cast the skin a sickly orange. Rostnikov wanted to be gone before that light came to his wife's face, but he knew he would not leave till she ordered him to do so.

"Are you all right?" she asked.

"I was thinking about balloons," he said. "Iosef was never interested in balloons."

Sarah smiled. He returned the smile, and she took his hand the way the little girl had done half a century ago. He looked at her and thought that in the evening light and shadow she looked, with her bandaged head and white gown, like a little girl playing a role, perhaps the role of a wise Gypsy fortune teller.

"But Iosef loved the circus," she said.

In the next bed, the girl Petra Toverinin dozed, a book lying open on her stomach. Irinia Komistok, the old woman, was off somewhere receiving therapy. Porfiry and Sarah were as alone as they probably ever would be in the hospital.

"What about that man?" Sarah asked, trying to sit up a bit.

"Bulgarin," Rostnikov said. "Ivan Bulgarin. He is gone. His family removed him from the hospital yesterday."

"Where did they take him?"

Rostnikov shrugged. "I'll find out, but not today. I couldn't push the balloon too hard or it might break," he said.

"It doesn't matter," Sarah said, sounding tired. "If he has a family taking care of him."

"I'll find out nonetheless," he said.

The girl in the next bed stirred and the book slipped from her stomach to the floor in a flutter like a landing bird. The sound struck something in Rostnikov.

"Porfiry?" Sarah said. "What is it?"

"The American writer Edgar Allan Poe," he said, softly squeezing her hand. "He said that melancholy is the path of beauty."

"I think you are tired," said Sarah. "Why don't you go home, lift your weights, read a little, and get something to eat."

"Yes," Rostnikov agreed, both reluctant and eager to go. If she were better, would he share with her, tell her where Ivan Bulgarin, the bear who had burst into her room, was leading him? No doubt he should drop the whole thing, forget that Nahatchavanski's name had been given to him by Lukov at the Lentaka Shoe Factory. But perhaps he could pursue it just a bit further to satisfy his curiosity. Besides, he was curious about why Bulgarin was suddenly removed from the hospital and why no record of his transfer could be found.

Rostnikov let go of his wife's hand and massaged his leg with both hands before standing up. Then he moved to the side of the sleeping girl's bed, picked up the fallen book, and placed it on the small table nearby.

"Tomorrow," he said, turning to his wife to kiss her forehead, which felt moist and slightly feverish. "Are you all right?"

"Fine," she said. "It takes time. You have vegetables?"

"Potatoes," he said.

"Find something green," she said. "Eat something green. Promise."

"I promise," he answered, touching her hand and moving to the door and opening it as the last light of day faded. "You want the lights on?"

"No," she said. "I think I'll sleep."

"Tomorrow," he said.

"If you're too busy . . ." she began, following through on the ritual they had established after his first visit.

"I'm not too busy," he said, closing the door behind him.

Chapter Nine

When Rostnikov arrived at Petrovka the next morning, the sun was not yet up. The armed uniformed guard inside the door stood behind a plastic shield, his machine pistol at the ready. His eyes met Rostnikov's with recognition and returned to the front door.

The sixth floor was not exactly bustling with activity, but neither was it absolutely quiet. A trio of inspectors was using one of the glass-enclosed rooms. Their heads were close together, and they looked tired. One, a man known as Walchek the Pole, was shaking his head no while the others entreated. Walchek looked up when Rostnikov passed and nodded.

Karpo at his desk, pen in hand preparing a report, did not turn around when Rostnikov entered his office, but Rostnikov knew he had been noticed. Tkach and Zelach arrived almost an hour later, Tkach looking tired, Zelach silent and slouching. When the four men met in Rostnikov's

141

small office moments later, Porfiry Petrovich was lost in thought and concentrating on a sketch he was making of neat tubes of various sizes connected in an intricate pattern.

"Reports," he said, putting a final touch of shading on a tube and standing up.

Karpo and Tkach placed filled-in forms on the desk, and Rostnikov glanced at them.

"And now," he said, "tell me what is not in these reports."

"The man who was found shot, Tolvenovov," Tkach said, "was killed on a bus, probably our missing bus, probably by Turkistani separatists, probably led by a man in his late forties. If we find the man, Kostnitsov can positively identify him through DNA. The dead man grabbed the man's wrist."

"*When* you find him, Sasha, *when*, not *if*," said Rostnikov, leaning forward, hands on the back of his chair. "To say *if* is to prepare yourself for defeat. So what will you do to catch him, Sasha?"

"Computer," said Tkach, holding back a yawn. "Identify and locate Turkistani separatists or those who know the Turkistani community, try to get a lead if it was Turkistanis."

Tkach was seated in the corner, Zelach standing behind him. Karpo stood in the other corner.

"You had trouble sleeping, Sasha?" Rostnikov asked.

"My mother," he said, brushing his hair back. "She . . . we talked most of the night."

Outside the cubicle the sixth floor was coming to life. A pair of uniformed officers flanked a smiling man whom they jostled forward between the desks and toward the room where Walchek the Pole and the other two investigators were still seated. The prisoner was ridiculously thin and looked as if he had some disease.

Rostnikov grunted and looked at Karpo.

"I believe Yuri Vostoyavek and a young girl are planning to murder Andrei Morchov," Karpo said.

Zelach shuffled in his corner and Rostnikov picked up Karpo's report. There was nothing about a conspiracy to commit murder in the report because, as Karpo had just said, he "believed" but did not know. He would not put his beliefs in a report, only his certainties. Besides, if his beliefs seemed to be well founded, the case would be taken from the Wolfhound's investigative team. As it was, Karpo was only investigating the probable hysterical reaction of a mother to her son's almost certainly innocent comment. By the same token, Tkach was investigating the disappearance of a bus, not an unrelated murder. The bus was probably, according to the report that would be filed, taken by an alcoholic bus driver who would soon be found asleep in some field.

"And what shall we do about our young would-be assassins?" Rostnikov asked Karpo.

"We can bring them in for questioning," said Karpo. "But I do not think they will confess. It will simply make them bide their time and make a greater effort to have the crime look like an accident. Nor do I think it will do any good to confront Comrade Morchov again. We can watch, be alert, and catch them in the act or just before the act."

"Just before the act would be far better," suggested Rostnikov. "Let us try that. And let us find out why this young man may wish to kill a member of the

Politburo and who the young woman is who may share his goal."

Karpo nodded and left the room.

"Very good," said Rostnikov with a deep sigh. "I am pursuing the possibility of petty theft in the Lentaka Shoe Factory. There is an office in the factory that I would like to examine tonight, but it is of vital importance that no one know in advance what I will be doing. I should like two volunteers to aid me in this."

Tkach nodded in agreement, and Karpo simply blinked his eyes in acceptance. Both knew that there must be something more to this assignment than catching a petty thief, but neither man would think of asking what it might be. They were better off not knowing, or Rostnikov would now be explaining.

"Good. Pursue your work and meet me at eleven-thirty tonight in front of the Tass building," Rostnikov said. "Zelach, would you please go process an order for level two computer access? I will get Colonel Snitkonoy to approve it. Sasha, remain a moment."

Karpo left the room and moved to his desk.

"Sasha Tkach," Rostnikov said gently, "if you do not sleep nights, you cannot work days, and ours is a job where being alert may mean staying alive. You have much to live for."

Tkach looked up but slouched back in his chair.

"My mother is making me feel guilty about the move," he explained. "She weeps, she complains, she goes silent, she threatens, she casts looks. She wakes the baby. Pulcharia is a good child, but ... And Maya, Maya who has always been so gentle, so quiet and loving, is becoming ... I'm caught between."

"I can't have you caught between or feeling caught between," said Rostnikov. "There is a murdered man, a missing bus and driver, more crimes taking place every day."

"I know," Tkach said with exhaustion before he nodded and left the room.

When Tkach was back at his desk, Rostnikov reached for the phone and checked his watch. He had ten minutes before his morning meeting with the Wolfhound. Rostnikov got the operator and asked for the Ministry of Information. Moments later he asked for and got Lydia Tkach on the line.

"You remember me?" he asked when she shouted *"Zdrah'stvooit'e,"* hello, into the phone.

"Yes!" she screamed. "What do you want? I'm very busy!"

Rostnikov moved the phone a foot away from his ear and returned it only when she was not speaking.

"Children," he said, "are ungrateful creatures. Your son is an ungrateful creature."

"You think I don't know that?" she said with a bitter laugh. "I needed you to call me from my work to tell me what I already know."

"Sasha, my son Iosef, all of them ungrateful," Rostnikov said.

"Tell *him* that," she cried. "He won't listen to me."

"He is beyond reason," Rostnikov said with a sigh. "I can't get him to do a decent day's work. All he thinks about, talks about, is you, his poor mother for whom he is trying to do his best. I've done much for him, Lydia Tkach. I've treated him like my own son, but if he doesn't start working, doesn't start showing some gratitude for all I've done, doesn't stop putting your feelings and wel-

145

fare above his duty to the State, I'll have to consider asking him to leave the service."

"Leave the—" she began.

"For his own good," said Rostnikov, sighing. "I must leave now. Your son is sitting at his desk with his head in his hands and not getting his work done."

"I'm deaf, Rostnikov, not stupid!" she shouted. "My son would not sit at his desk like a whipped child. Don't call and play games with me."

"He is a good man and I need him," said Rostnikov. "And he is a good son. And you need him. Think about it, Lydia Tkach, and we'll talk about it at lunch. I'll come for you at two."

"You can't bribe me out of my apartment with a bowl of soup and a blini!" she bellowed.

"Think about it," he repeated.

"I can get off for lunch at one, not two," she said in a nearly normal tone.

"Good-bye," he said.

When he hung up the receiver, Rostnikov knew he would have to hurry to make the Wolfhound's morning meeting. He hoped the meeting would be brief.

―――――――――

The computer came up with several names and places for Zelach and Sasha Tkach. There was the new Center for Turkistani Culture. There was a prisoner in Lubyanka who was suspected of robbing a couple on the Metro. When arrested he claimed to be liberating the money to make bombs to demonstrate the seriousness of Turkistani cultural identity. Of course, the young man was drunk when arrested, but he was being held nonetheless. There were other names. Tkach made a printout and signed for it. He gave Zelach half the names and took half for himself. It would be faster this way, though Sasha had no confidence in Zelach asking the right questions. If Sasha turned up no leads, he would have to go back and check Zelach's list himself. He was not particularly sure of his own ability to do his own job, let alone Zelach's, without a bit of undisturbed sleep, but he felt a sense of urgency. What would Turkistani separatists want with a bus? Why would they want it so much that they would kill for it? And why would they want a bus driver?

Three hours later, he had talked to the young man in prison, who proved to be a braggart, a drunk, and a fool. Three other leads proved to be useless and, what is worse, quite distant from each other.

By one in the afternoon, Sasha wanted to think, to wake up. The afternoon was brisk, cool, and threatening, once again, to rain. He walked down to Petrovka Street past the Bolshoi Theater's eight tall stuccoed columns, atop which stood four rearing horses harnessed to the chariot of Apollo. He crossed Marx Prospekt to the garden in front of the 220-ton monument to Karl Marx, which had been officially completed and shown on Sasha's sixth birthday. Lydia, he remembered, had brought him down for the unveiling of the great man, who leaned eternally against a stone rostrum as if in midspeech, while below him were engraved his words of revolution, "Workers of the world, unite."

Beyond Sverdlov Square he glanced at the old Central Lenin Museum and moved down into the huge underground connection to the Revolution Square, Sverdlov Square, and Prospekt Marksa Metro stations. Ten minutes later he stepped out of the Volgograd Prospekt Station, found a small café where he had two coffees in the hope that they would wake him up, and made his way to the run-down concrete building that housed the Center for Turkistani Culture and dozens of other offices, causes, and businesses that awaited a moment of respect or recognition that might never come.

The Center for Turkistani Culture, as it turned out, consisted of two mismatched desks, one of metal with rust creeping through the thin layer of paint, the other of battered wood. A quartet of wooden chairs stood in the corner of the room, with a table in the middle where two very old men, one of whom was turning out billows of gray smoke from an ancient and foul-smelling pipe, were playing a game of chess.

Behind one of the desks sat a very dark woman who was neither young nor old nor very interested in the visitor. She wore a serious dark dress that came up to her collar and a more serious, short, no-nonsense hair style. She looked very Greek to Sasha, who showed his identification card.

"So you are a policeman," she said, apparently unimpressed, her hands folded.

"Are you here to return our country to us?" said the old chess player with the pipe. The other man grunted.

A year ago such talk to a policeman could have been enough for a journey to Petrovka. It was still not the safest thing to do even in a mad world, but Sasha was too tired for such games.

"I'm looking for some men and a woman," he said,

addressing the woman behind the desk. "Possibly a group of young people and an older man. Turkistanis who may have some knowledge of a crime."

"Not much to go on," the woman said.

Sasha suddenly felt like a schoolchild in front of his teacher. Yes, the woman looked like a teacher.

"If these people commit a crime, your cause will be set back," Sasha tried.

Both old men laughed, and the one who had spoken before removed the pipe from his mouth and spoke again. "A cause that has gotten nowhere cannot be set back."

"It can be destroyed," said Sasha.

"Threats?" said the old man, now looking up from the board.

"Play," said the other man irritably. "Play the game. Mind your business, Ivan."

"No threats," Sasha said, holding up his hands and smiling boyishly.

"We know of no one like that," said the woman.

"They may have killed a man yesterday," Sasha pressed on, feeling that the woman did know something, did have an idea. The possibility woke him, made him alert.

"Unfortunate," said the woman. "I have much work to do here. If you would please leave, I would—"

"A name, a name from any of you," Sasha said. "No one will know where I got it, and the police would be in your debt."

"In our debt?" the old man named Ivan said. "How much in our debt?"

"We cannot pay for information," Sasha said, turning to the old man, who made a move that the other old man quickly pounced upon.

"A permit to hold a meeting," Ivan said.

"Ivan," the woman behind the desk warned.

"Donkey shit," said Ivan, pointing his pipe at her. "I'm eighty-two years old. What are they going to do to me? Kill me? I give him a name. Maybe some people we can't talk to reasonably get sent away by the police, and we get a permit to meet. What do you say, police boy?"

"I say let me make a phone call," he replied.

"And I say," said Ivan, "tell me now. I've just lost this game to this, this piss-hill dwarf, and I want to get out of here and get a drink."

"I don't have the authority," Sasha said.

"Then you don't get a name," said old Ivan, standing up and putting on a frayed cap.

"I'll get you a permit," he said.

"Ivan," said the woman with a sigh, "you are a fool."

"And we are going to have a permit," he said with a grin that revealed an almost toothless mouth.

"You trust this policeman?" the woman said, looking at Sasha.

"Why not?" Ivan said with a shrug. "What we have to lose? Tell him the name, Lavrenti."

The other old man got off his chair, and Sasha saw that he was indeed nearly a dwarf.

"You won the game," said Ivan. "Now tell the boy who he is looking for."

"Peotor Kotsis," said the little man.

"Peotor Kotsis," Sasha repeated.

"Where did you hear that name?" asked Ivan.

"Where did I . . . he just . . ." And Sasha understood. "Someone called in with a tip," Sasha said, looking at the woman, who pretended to be busy with her papers.

"What did we tell you?" Ivan asked.

"I don't recall," said Sasha. "What would this caller tell me about how to find Peotor Kotsis?"

"Who knows?" said Ivan, putting his hand on the little man's shoulder. The two shuffled to the door and left.

"You're not going to get a permit for us, are you?" the woman said.

"I will get the permit," Sasha said, anxious to leave. "I will get the permit."

"The man on the phone. The one who called you? He told you to look for a girl named Sonia selling flowers on the Arbat."

"A girl named Sonia," Sasha repeated. "Where on the Arbat?"

"How would I know?" the woman said without looking up. "He called you, not me."

The Gray Wolfhound sat behind his desk, back straight, afternoon sun catching his distinct, etched profile. He wore a brown uniform with only three medals, but those medals caught the sun, and their reflections danced on the walls of the semidarkened room. The Wolfhound read the reports in front of him slowly, muttering an occasional "hmm" or "ah" as he turned the pages.

Rostnikov had decided to stand rather than sit, though the colonel had suggested that he make himself comfortable. If it took the Wolfhound five more minutes, Rostnikov would have to sit. The ache would come and he would have to relieve it. He had sat through a full hour of Major

Grigorovich explaining parade routes. And then Pankov had stumbled over a financial report. When they had left, the Wolfhound had asked Rostnikov to stay so the colonel could more closely examine the current cases under investigation.

Colonel Snitkonoy put down the reports and looked up at his investigator. But still he did not speak. He put the tips of his long fingers together, tapping them lightly twice. "You know what is happening in China, Porfiry Petrovich?" he said finally.

"I've heard of unrest," Rostnikov said, his eyes meeting those of the Wolfhound's.

"Unrest, yes," said the colonel. "It is speculated that the reforms in our country provided the model for the Chinese response. Do you think that likely?"

There was usually, but not always, a point to the colonel's seemingly random observations.

"According to Engels, all things are possible that fall within the range of scientific probability and the laws of nature," said Rostnikov. It was not, in fact, Porfiry Petrovich's operative philosophy, but it was one of the acceptable responses. One could, and sometimes did, get through life by engaging in a prescribed dialogue founded upon clichés drawn from Marx, Engels, Lenin, and the latest acceptable interpreter of revolutionary truth.

"There are people, people in our government who are especially sensitive at the present time," said the Wolfhound, rising, two hands open flat on the table. "What we do impacts on the world. One small error, scandal, indication of hypocrisy on the part of our government and our credibility will be seriously undermined."

Rostnikov was beginning to see what was coming. It

had happened before. He had handled it before, but not always to his own satisfaction. Someone wanted him to stop probing.

"Find your thief at the shoe factory," the Wolfhound said. "Deal with the hysterical woman and her son. Find the bus. If you find more than a shoe thief, a bragging son, and a drunken bus driver, deal with the situation, but deal with it within the bounds outlined in your reports. These are tender times for me and those who work for me. Trouble wears many disguises. Unmask it carefully, Comrade Inspector."

"I will," said Rostnikov.

"Good," said the Wolfhound with a sigh, indicating that this phase of the conversation was over. He stepped around from behind his desk, put his hands behind his back, and walked to the window. "Did you know that Deputy Andrei Morchov is a friend of mine?"

"I did not know," said Rostnikov.

"I'll say nothing to him when I see him tonight at the reception for the Chinese cultural envoy," said the Wolfhound, gazing out at the quickly dropping sun. "But if he asks me about the investigation, I will tell him that it appears to be nothing but the absurdity of a headstrong youth."

"That would seem reasonable," Rostnikov agreed.

"And I would like the deputy to be undisturbed in the future over so slight a matter," the colonel added.

"I will see to it that Deputy Morchov is undisturbed over slight matters," Rostnikov agreed.

"I am going to confide in you, Porfiry Petrovich," the Wolfhound said, still looking out the window. There were no lights on in the room, and the walls were fast disap-

153

pearing. Rostnikov was not sure that he wanted the colonel's confidence.

"My position is largely ceremonial," the Wolfhound said. "I know that. You know that. Ceremony is essential in a state in which people who represent us are often without . . ."

"Presence," Rostnikov supplied.

"Presence, yes," the colonel agreed. "And dignity. And pride."

Rostnikov thought he detected a smile in the corner of the famous profile.

"I've made few if any enemies, Porfiry Petrovich. I am permitted an investigative staff, your staff, consisting of personnel who are not wanted in other departments but, for reasons I cannot always fathom, are too valuable simply to dismiss. We are permitted to function, investigate as long as we remain harmless, unthreatening to other investigative bodies. I'll not ask you if you understand where I am going with this. You are always well ahead of me."

"I'm not—" Rostnikov began.

"I have neither the time nor the disposition to listen to false modesty," the Wolfhound said with a deep sigh. "I do not possess modesty, and I do not admire it in others. My political future is suddenly very promising, Porfiry Petrovich. If I—we—do not stumble. If the reforms continue, we may emerge with more than a ceremonial image. You understand?"

Colonel Snitkonoy turned, his face now hidden by shadows, and Rostnikov nodded.

"Good," the colonel said. "Be careful. Since you have joined my staff, you and your associates, we have attracted attention, a new respect, but respect has a price. Be careful, Porfiry Petrovich. I'm late. I'm to be at the reception in one hour."

"One last thing, Colonel," Rostnikov said, taking the requisition form from his pocket and flattening it on the colonel's desk. "I would appreciate your signature so I can obtain a few items to complete a minor investigation."

The colonel moved to Rostnikov's side and looked down at the requisition. He read the list and looked at Rostnikov.

"An automobile for the night," he said. "A French folding ladder. A portable battery-operated copying machine. And a—"

"I can explain," said Rostnikov.

"Do I want to hear the explanation?" asked the colonel.

"Probably not," Rostnikov said.

"Then I will allow my curiosity to give way to self-interest." He signed his name with a flourish. "Be careful, Porfiry Petrovich."

The colonel looked down at his watch, turning his wrist to catch the last of the sun. The cue was clear, and Rostnikov headed for the door, opened it gently, and stepped into the light of the outer office, closing the colonel's door gently behind him.

"The lights are out," said Pankov, the colonel's assistant, greeting Rostnikov at the door.

"Yes," said Rostnikov, moving past the tiny man who patted the few strands of hair on his head in a fruitless effort to make them behave less willfully.

"He has had something on his mind for days," said Pankov.

"It would seem," Rostnikov agreed.

"Is he . . . in a mood?" Pankov asked, looking at the Wolfhound's door.

Yes, the Wolfhound was in a mood, but what the mood was had been difficult for Rostnikov to determine. It was as if the colonel had a piece of information, something to say, something he could not bring himself to convey or was unable to speak. Rostnikov had been sure that he or one of his men was going to be warned off of an investigation, but the warning had not come, and that disturbed Rostnikov. A direct warning would make sense and could be dealt with.

"He is in a mood," Rostnikov said, looking back at the obviously frightened man. "But an introspective one, a benevolent one."

"He can—" Pankov began with a wary smile, but the smile and thought were erased by the colonel's deep voice bellowing through the inner door.

"Pankov!" called the Wolfhound.

Pankov patted down his hair and hurried for the Wolfhound's door, forgetting the inspector, who left the office with a requisition for the items he would need that night to break into the offices of the Lentaka Shoe Factory.

―――――

At the very moment, or close to it, that Pankov opened the door of Colonel Snitkonoy's office and found himself in almost total darkness, four people entered an equally darkened barn in a wooded area on the outskirts of the town of Klin.

The four people were Boris Trush the bus driver, Peotor

and Vasily Kotsis, and an Oriental-looking young woman of clear features who said nothing and wore a knowing smile.

Boris had sat in the backseat of the Volga between Peotor and Vasily, while the unnamed woman drove. There was not enough room in the backseat for three people. Thigh pressed against thigh. Garlic, tobacco, and sweat enclosed Boris, who was wearing worn farming clothes. The clothes were too large and smelled bad. Boris's sweating and the proximity of his captors did not improve the situation.

And all the way to Klin, as they drove along the Leningrad Highway for more than fifty miles, Peotor waxed on about the history of the area.

"Boris, Comrade," Peotor said confidentially, "I was a teacher of music. A teacher of music. And history. We are making a historic journey."

Vasily reached down and checked the automatic rifle in his lap. Something clicked. Boris shuddered. Peotor paused and then continued, "The town of Klin was founded in 1318. A beautiful town on the high bank of the Sestra River." He turned to look out the window at the rows of birch trees. "Have you ever been there, Boris?"

"No," said Boris.

Vasily smiled at him.

"There are two impressive old churches in Klin, one built in the sixteenth century and another in 1712, both quite different in design. We may catch a glimpse of the newer church, baroque, not my preference. But it is not the churches that people go to Klin to see."

"Tchaikovsky," Boris muttered, his voice dry, cracking.

"Yes," said Peotor, turning to look at the bus driver with a touch of respect.

"Tchaikovsky's house still stands, unchanged, as it was, a museum," Peotor said softly. "The Nazis occupied Klin in 1941, brutalized the house, but it was restored."

"We can't stop at museums," Vasily said.

"I say where we stop," Peotor responded gently. Vasily grunted.

"Who says where we stop, Boris? Tell my son," Peotor said, pressing the issue.

"You do," Boris said, unwilling to be in the middle of a battle between father and son.

"You do," Vasily agreed with a sigh.

Peotor reached past Boris's face to slap his son playfully.

"It is in Klin Pyotr Ilich composed *Sleeping Beauty*, the Fifth and Sixth symphonies, *Hamlet*, *The Nutcracker*. Of Klin, Tchaikovsky once wrote, 'I can't imagine myself anywhere else. I find no words to express how much I feel the charm of the Russian countryside, the Russian landscape, and this stillness that I need more than anything else.' "

"Beautiful," said Vasily sarcastically.

Peotor chose to ignore his son and, to Boris's relief, said, "Our country can have this tranquillity, this sense of history, identity restored. We can do this, Boris."

"We can," Boris agreed. "Why are we going—?"

"Patience," said Peotor.

"Shut up," whispered Vasily.

The woman driving the car giggled slightly.

And then they had come to Klin. Well, not quite to Klin. Just beyond it, to the barn down a narrow wooded road. There was a clearing, and on the left a few stone remnants of what had once probably been a great house. On the right was the barn, which looked reasonably sturdy. Stone and wood, it stood silently as Peotor, Vasily, Boris, and the woman climbed out.

"Here," Vasily said, putting something in the right hand of Boris, who walked forward between the father and son, who both wore long coats, as did the woman. The woman walked slightly behind them. "Into your pocket," Vasily whispered.

Boris obeyed and walked with them to the barn door, which Peotor opened into near darkness.

"Stop," came a voice from somewhere deep inside the barn.

The quartet stopped and Peotor spoke.

Someone threw open a wooden window that clattered, shook, and let in a bit of twilight, not enough to see faces but enough for Boris to see figures, perhaps five of them.

"You have it?" came the voice that had first spoken. It seemed to come from a large, outlined figure to the left.

"In the trunk of the car," said Peotor.

"Let's look," said the voice.

"Let us first see the weapons," said Peotor.

A muffled conversation went on in the darkness between the large figure and another, slighter figure.

"Step forward, alone," the large figure said.

Peotor nodded and stepped forward. A flashlight came on and pointed to a table against the wall. Four large suitcases stood on the table. The suitcases were old, of different colors. The light caught metal in the suitcases as Peotor advanced and examined the contents.

Boris tried to penetrate the darkness but could see nothing and only heard the pleased humming of Vasily.

After a long minute and the sound of metal clanking and the tunnel of light from the flashlight bouncing from suitcase to suitcase, Peotor turned.

"All right," he said.

Vasily's humming got louder, and the Oriental woman stepped up next to Boris.

"Good. Let's see the money and get out of here," said the large figure.

"No money," said Peotor. "Not that kind of money. We can't afford it. We need it for living. A revolution is expensive, and we have too few friends. But we do have something of greater value for you."

"No money, no weapons," the man in the dark said angrily.

And then a flash and a boom, a cacophony that echoed through the barn, causing a sonic boom in Boris's head, but that was only the beginning. At his side, Vasily lifted his automatic weapon and began firing. People tried to scurry, but there was nowhere to go. A figure went for the open window and was torn by a fresh burst from Vasily. At Boris's side, the Oriental woman prodded him. She had a handgun and was firing into a corner at something that may or may not have been human.

"Shoot," she said with a hiss. Boris pulled his hand from his pocket, and in it was a pistol he could barely see. Behind them the barn door opened. Boris turned. A woman, perhaps a boy, stood in outline like a perfect cutout. In the hand of the woman-boy was a shotgun. Without thought, Boris Trush fired at the figure and wet his pants at the same time. The figure fell as the noise of death and weapons throbbed through Boris's head.

And then all was silent.

In the heartbeat of that instant of silence, Boris considered turning his gun on the Oriental girl, on Vasily, on Peotor, but before the instant had throbbed he knew he could not do it. He might kill one of them, but the others would turn him into one of the lifeless, bloody creatures that lay in the darkness around him.

"Vasily?" Peotor's voice called from the darkness.

"Yes."

"Lia?"

"Yes," the woman replied.

"Boris?"

Boris could not speak. He looked down at the dead figure in the doorway.

"Boris?" Peotor repeated impatiently.

"Yes," Boris answered.

Someone moaned near the table. Another shot.

"Good," said Peotor. "Let's do this."

Boris could see a bit better now with the door open, but he did not want to see. Peotor closed each of the suitcases and handed one to Vasily and the woman. He took one himself and held one out for Boris, who could not move.

"Boris," Peotor said firmly, and Boris shuffled forward, stepping over the large dead man near the table, taking the suitcase.

And then they were back in the car. Vasily had taken the pistol back from Boris. The suitcases had been placed in the trunk.

Boris needed a change of clothes, but it took him a moment to realize it. He was also afraid to say it, afraid Peotor would tell him to take the pants of one of the dead men.

As they pulled away, Boris looked back at the doorway

of the barn and told himself, It was a small man, not a boy, not a woman, a small man who would have killed me. A small man. But he was not sure.

"Hurry. I've got to get back to the city tonight. Wait. There," Peotor said as the woman hit the outer road. "Look. Against the sky. The old church. See it?"

Boris turned his head in the direction Peotor was looking. Perhaps he saw something. Perhaps not. Two days earlier he had simply been a bus driver.

Chapter Ten

Emil Karpo sat on the hard wooden chair in the darkened bedroom, considering what he would do if he resigned his position. He could think of nothing. He had spent his life till now serving the State. He existed to serve the State. He had no interests but the service of the State. His task was to locate those responsible for crimes and turn the criminals in for trial. Criminals were parasites draining the energy of communism. Emil Karpo was, at that moment, in need of a metaphor, but none came to mind. In fact, the "parasite" image was not his own but Karl Marx's. Karpo did not imagine a crawling or flying or slithering creature attacking a determined and noble bear named Russia. Emil Karpo had no imagination. He considered this his principal strength.

The person on the bed in front of Karpo stirred but did not awaken. Karpo watched unblinking, unmoving. Karpo had to be on a street corner more than two miles away in less than twenty minutes. If the figure in the bed did not awaken soon, Karpo would have to awaken him.

Because he had no imagination or had used it so little, Emil Karpo could not put words to his present feelings, though he knew his dilemma. His responsibility was to catch Yuri Vostoyavek and the girl in the act of conspiring to kill Andrei Morchov or to stop them as they were about to perform the act. Never before had Karpo's duty been so clear. Morchov was a key member of the Politburo.

Karpo did not want to admit to himself that he had disliked Morchov. That was not relevant. Should not be. Karpo did not want to admit that he could see the anguish, desperation on the faces of the girl and Yuri Vostoyavek. But Karpo was not easy on himself. He acknowledged these realizations and considered them threats to his effectiveness.

The penalty for conspiring to assassinate a member of the government was death.

"Huh," the figure in the bed grunted in the darkness, perhaps sensing another person in the room. He sat up, eyes blinking.

"Mother? What are you . . . ?" and then Yuri Vostoyavek knew that the outlined, straight-backed figure in the chair next to his bed was not his mother. It didn't even seem to be human.

"Who are . . ." Yuri began and then whirled and reached for a weapon, any weapon. His hand closed on the metal alarm clock on the table next to his bed. He jumped out of bed naked and breathing heavily as Karpo rose and caught the descending hand holding the clock. Yuri tried to punch at the skeleton face before him with his free hand, but that, too, was stopped by Karpo.

The boy did not scream. He was afraid. Karpo could feel that, had felt it many times before. Karpo could smell his fear, and the boy could smell a dry cleanliness on the night figure, a smell he immediately equated with death.

"He found out. He sent you," Yuri said, trying to control his breathing. "You're the one I saw this morning."

Karpo held the boy's hands so that he could not move. Their bodies were together. When Yuri had awakened and leaped from the bed, Karpo saw that he had an erection. The erection was gone now, but the boy was not limp.

"Then kill me," he whispered and dropped the clock.

The clock clattered to the floor, and a voice called from the next room. The voice of Elena Vostoyavek, Yuri's mother.

"Yuri, what . . . are you all right?"

Yuri's face was inches from Karpo, and his eyes were now sufficiently adjusted to the minimal light to see the unblinking, gaunt face before him.

"I'm fine," Yuri called. "I knocked over the clock."

"Yes," his mother called and went back to sleep.

"Then do it," he whispered to Karpo. "Do it and be sure it looks like murder. I don't want my mother and Jalna to think I was a coward."

"I'm not going to murder you," Karpo said. "I'm going to warn you. One warning. What you plan to do is known. Stop and it is the end. Stop, Yuri Vostoyavek, or it will be your end and that of the girl. You understand?"

Yuri looked at the emotionless face inches in front of him, tried to see the eyes in dark shadow, tried to understand what was happening and thought only that he had to get to the toilet, had to get there very quickly.

"I understand," Yuri said.

Karpo let him free and stood back.

"I was not here," Karpo said, stepping back into the dark corner of the small room, where there was a door that led to the hallway in front of the apartment. Karpo did not think about the name of the girl that Yuri had uttered. He did not have to think. He knew from the file he had carefully studied that Morchov's daughter was named Jalna. He knew that in the morning he would check to be sure that the girl who wanted Morchov dead was his own daughter. And he knew what he would find.

"I was not here," Karpo repeated softly.

Yuri nodded, not knowing if the dark figure was still there when he did so, not hearing a sound. And then Yuri headed for the toilet.

———————

Emil Karpo was not late. It was eleven twenty-one when he arrived in front of the Tass building just off of Koltso Boulevard. Rostnikov was sitting on a bench reading a book by the light of a streetlamp. Sasha had not yet come. The hour was late, the area deserted but for a pair of late-night lovers who crossed the street, moving toward the Church of the Ascension to avoid the strange pair of men who seemed to be waiting for a bus long after the buses had stopped running for the night.

Rostnikov put his book away, nodded at Karpo, and invited him to sit next to him on the bench. Karpo hesitated and then sat.

"I have a car," Rostnikov said. "Around the corner. It

must be back before dawn. What do you have, Emil Karpo?"

"What do I have? Nothing," said Karpo.

"You look like you have something, the memory of a nightmare or a bad conscience," said Rostnikov, shifting his weight. "Would you rather not join us tonight?"

"You believe you may need my assistance?"

"Yes."

"I will join you. If you sense a restiveness in me, it is not about what we will do tonight."

"The Morchov business," said Rostnikov with a sigh.

Karpo said nothing.

"Would you like me to take it over?"

"It is my responsibility," said Karpo firmly.

"Your responsibility is to see that, if possible, no one gets hurt," said Rostnikov. "The courts are crowded with cases. People sit in their homes, in cells waiting for a hearing on whether they stole a neighbor's potato pie or failed to meet a quota in their small factory. Our duty is often done best if we bring a case to conclusion without the need of a court."

Somewhere behind them came the sound of footsteps. They were soft, faint, and almost certain to be unheard by anyone not listening for them, anyone but a policeman. Both Karpo and Rostnikov heard the steps coming in their direction.

"A trial is the right of every citizen," Karpo said with less than his usual full conviction on such issues.

"It is a right that many citizens would gladly forgo if they could be given other options," said Rostnikov.

At this point Sasha came around the corner, breathing heavily.

"I'm late," he said.

"It gave me an opportunity to discuss the philosophy of the legal system with Emil," said Rostnikov, standing up.

"I was trying to find a woman in the Arbat who may be a lead to the missing bus and . . . that can wait," Sasha said. "I had to call Maya. I haven't been home."

"You want to go home?" Rostnikov said, reaching down to massage his leg. "Emil and I can continue our discussion and handle the situation."

"You said you might need me," said Sasha, brushing his hair back. He had not shaved since early this morning, and amber bristles on his cheeks caught the light from the streetlamp and, strangely, made him look even younger than usual.

"We might," Rostnikov said.

"Then let's go," said Sasha.

Moments later they were in the green four-door Moskvich Rostnikov had signed out from Petrovka. On his application for use, he had cited a stakeout to catch a factory thief. The garage clerk was not a dim fellow but he was not secure and would not question the authority of a superior unless the clerk was being watched. Zelach had driven Rostnikov and the car to the street just behind Tass and then had gone home on the Metro, as Rostnikov requested. Zelach had neither asked what was happening nor had appeared to have any curiosity about the matter.

Karpo drove. They had turned the corner and were a block away from where the car had been parked when the dark Chaika, its headlights off, began to follow them.

The Man Who Walked Like a Bear

Boris Trush lay on his cot in the run-down farmhouse beyond nowhere and tried to rid his mind of the repeating refrain of the childhood song, but it would not go away. It was better than the vision of the boy he was sure he had killed in Klin, but it was terrible nonetheless.

"In the field is standing a birch tree," it repeated over and over and over again. He knew that Tchaikovsky had used the song in some symphony or other. Boris didn't know or care much for music, but this he remembered.

He should not be thinking of songs. Boris wanted to think about escaping, wanted to think about the murder he had committed. No, no, he did not want to think about that. And, besides, it wasn't a murder. He didn't want to be there, in that barn, in this house. He wanted to be home in his bed, wanted to check his trip ticket for the morning, wanted to get up and have a strong cup of coffee and put on his uniform and drive his bus. Boris wanted his routine. He cared nothing for freedom. He wanted the comfort of his routine, not this song of birch trees, not this box of madness.

Beyond the wall and his song Boris could hear Vasily and the Oriental girl Lia grunting, rolling, laughing, bouncing. They murder and then they have sex. They have no routine, Boris thought. He hated them, envied them, wanted them to be quiet, wanted the song in his brain to cease so he could sleep. If the song would go away, if Vasily and the girl would stop their games, Boris could sleep and then he could awaken refreshed, ready to make a plan.

"Not with that. I don't like that," the girl's voice came faintly through the wall. She sounded playful, unafraid.

"You'll like it," said Vasily. "Believe me."

"You're sure?" she said.

"I'm always sure," said Vasily.

Boris looked across the room into the darkness, where one of the young men in the group slept or pretended to sleep. He considered getting up, going to the window. He could not get through the door.

Boris had not seen Peotor Kotsis since they returned from the horror at Klin. He had simply said that he would be gone for a while and disappeared. Boris wasn't sure if he felt better or worse with Kotsis around. As insane as he seemed to be, Vasily was even more mad.

Just before he turned off the lights, the young man watching Boris had moved his own bed to block the door, but there was a window. If he could only think. No, not the window. The wooden floor creaked with each step night or day, and the window had not been opened since they had arrived. Perhaps it couldn't open? Even if it could, it would make noise. But . . . the girl beyond the wall laughed. She kills and laughs.

Boris began to sit up. He was shaking, damp with sweat though the night was cool.

"No," came a voice through the darkness.

"I need to—" Boris said.

"No," came the voice again.

"But I can't—" Boris said with a sigh.

The young man guarding him didn't even bother to answer. Boris lay back to the sound of passion beyond the wall and the birch tree song inside him.

The Man Who Walked Like a Bear

———————

There were four dogs and two guards at the Lentaka Shoe Factory. The dogs roamed the inside of the factory throughout the night, during which they were given no food. In the morning, before the first workers arrived, the dogs were rounded up by the guards, fed, and taken away to a massive kennel to join hundreds of other animals from hundreds of factories, stores, warehouses, concert halls, and museums.

Rostnikov expected the dogs. He also expected the guards. It would have been no problem to incapacitate the animals and the guards, but Rostnikov preferred, if at all possible, to give no indication of their visit. If Lukov, the manager of the factory, was telling the truth, a break-in might well alert those who were involved in the corruption, and once alerted, they might stop Rostnikov before he could act.

The plan was simple. Rostnikov had obtained upon requisition with the signature of Colonel Snitkonoy the car, a collapsible ladder, and a compact and portable battery-operated copying machine, a large, square box he handled with great care. He had also prepared a small box of tools. He had wrapped each tool individually in cloth to keep them from making noise. He had placed all these things gently in the trunk of the car before he had asked Zelach to drive him. In his pocket Rostnikov carried a rough map he had drawn showing the location of Lukov's office and that of Raya Corspoyva. He had given copies of the map to both Karpo and Tkach to study after they had parked down the street from the Lentaka Shoe Factory.

They had watched the factory for two hours and discovered that the guards had a simple, slovenly routine. Every half hour they would walk out the front door together and go in opposite directions, circling the entire factory and meeting again in front. The circuit took a little over eleven minutes. That would give Rostnikov, Karpo, and Tkach twenty minutes to get into the factory and back to the car.

The moment the guards made their fourth circuit, Karpo had, with lights out, driven quickly down a road to the right of the factory. The fence that surrounded the factory was no problem. It had not been designed as a serious deterrent but as a warning. There wasn't even barbed wire across the top of the fence, but that did not surprise the policemen. Barbed wire, which was really of little value in keeping out a determined burglar, sent a message that something of value was beyond the fence.

Within seconds of their arrival, Karpo had the ladder out of the trunk and over the fence. The ladder, an ingenious French device that could be set in various patterns, was locked to straddle the fence. Sasha Tkach, carrying the toolbox that Rostnikov had handed him, hurried over the ladder, followed by Karpo, who carried the large metal box with a handle. Rostnikov, for whom the task would be monumental even if he were not carrying a copying machine, albeit a very compact battery-operated one, came last. Rostnikov did not even attempt to use his left leg. He pulled himself up by one powerful arm, using his right leg as a guiding rudder. When they were all within the grounds of the factory, Rostnikov put down the machine and pulled the ladder over, collapsing it into a compact square, which he handed to Karpo.

The Man Who Walked Like a Bear

When they reached the outer wall of the factory, Rostnikov checked his watch. Four of their twenty minutes were gone. Leading the way, Rostnikov came to the window he knew to be Lukov's. It was, as he expected, locked. With Tkach watching in one direction and Karpo in the other, Rostnikov took his toolbox from Tkach, removed the proper instruments, and began quickly, efficiently to remove a pane of glass from the window. It took him but fifteen seconds. Karpo reached in and opened the latch. Then he slid the window up slowly, cautiously, almost noiselessly, but not noiselessly enough. Inside, beyond the door to Lukov's office, they could hear the dogs stirring, sensing something but not yet sure of it. Karpo unsnapped the ladder, quickly formed it, and put it through the open window.

Tkach scrambled up the ladder and through the window. Karpo handed him the two boxes and the machine and climbed through after him. Outside, Rostnikov closed the window and immediately began to replace the windowpane, while Karpo, using a small flashlight, moved to the files in the corner and, using a thin, flat piece of metal, opened the lock and began to search for the name Rostnikov had given him.

Beyond Lukov's office the dogs were now alert. In the dim night-lights of the factory, the policemen could see the animals sniffing the air and could hear their low growls. Almost seven minutes had passed.

Sasha knelt at the door with the large box on the floor next to him. Something moved in the box. Something inside let out a low, angry squeal.

The quick-drying putty he had used was already hardening when Rostnikov began to rub it with dark polish to make it match the other panes.

As he did so, the dogs went wild and headed for Lukov's office. Sasha opened the door, flipped open the large box, and instantly closed the door as Karpo turned off his flashlight and Rostnikov pulled himself through the window over the ladder. As the badger that Sasha had released scrambled across the factory floor and leaped upon a stack of synthetic leather, Rostnikov pulled the ladder in and closed the window.

Beyond the door the dogs barked. The badger hissed and barked back. One of the dogs in a frenzy crashed into a sewing machine, sending it clattering on the concrete floor. Peeking over the window in Lukov's door, Rostnikov saw the two guards rush in. One guard was short, old. The other massive, young, and carrying a gun.

Their voices carried through the door but not their words. The old man shouted at the dogs. The young man shouted at the old man and moved past him, seeing the badger on the pile of false leather.

"What is that?" the young man asked the old one.

"A thing," said the old man.

The badger saw the man with the gun and dug its claws into the material beneath its feet, sending the top sheet of material sliding behind him. The badger lost its grip and came flying onto the back of one of the dogs. The dog screamed and began to run madly around the factory, the badger clinging to him, the other dogs yelping. The massive young guard fired wildly, missing the badger but taking the left ear off of one of the dogs. The dog squealed in pain and turned on the young guard, who backed into a sewing machine.

The old man was confused, uncertain. The young man took aim and shot the attacking dog with the bloody ear as it was running at him.

The badger now leaped from the dog, leaving bloody patches on its back.

"The dog!" the old man clearly shouted. "You didn't have to shoot him! Shoot that thing!"

"I know, you fool!" screamed the massive young guard, ready to shoot the other dogs if they decided to attack.

The old man moved forward, petting the frightened dogs, comforting the whimpering, wounded animal. He led the frightened and now docile animals toward the door through which he and the massive guard had entered. One of the unwounded dogs turned his head for a final less-than-enthusiastic growl in the direction in which the badger had fled.

"So," the old man shouted, "go, take your gun and shoot that thing instead of some innocent dog!"

"I will!" the massive man shouted back.

And the old man led the dogs out, closing the door behind him.

Now the young guard was alone, or thought he was alone, with a dangerous unknown animal, an animal that the guard was afraid might be the more intelligent of the two.

The guard moved cautiously forward, heard a sound to his right, and decided to retreat through the door, which he closed firmly behind him.

The moment he was gone, Rostnikov, Karpo and Tkach were up.

If the guards went back to their normal rounds, the policemen had twelve minutes to complete their task. Karpo moved back to the files with his flashlight. Rostnikov opened the door to the office and with Tkach holding the box stepped into the factory. Rostnikov moved instantly to his right toward the office of Raya Corspoyva, and Tkach opened a heavily wrapped cow's heart that Rostnikov had carried in his toolbox.

Ten minutes later, the badger was safely in the box with his well-earned piece of meat and the three men were climbing out of the window of Lukov's office.

Rostnikov had just closed the window when they heard the voices of the two guards arguing loudly in front of the building.

There was no way they could get across the open field to the fence, get the ladder up, and be over before the guard turned the corner. Neither was there time to open the window and get back into the factory.

"Wait," Rostnikov whispered, motioning them back against the wall.

Karpo held the ladder. Tkach held the box with the badger. Rostnikov handed Karpo the copier and the toolbox and moved to the corner of the building as quickly as he could. He stood back in the shadows as the young guard mumbled to himself.

As the guard turned the corner, Rostnikov stepped behind him and grasped him in a bear hug. The man struggled, grunted, and tried to shout, but though he was a head taller than Rostnikov, he couldn't escape the older man's grip. They danced away from the wall in a circle. Rostnikov lifted the man and squeezed, squeezed until his hands went numb, squeezed ignoring the hands and nails that tore at his fingers, squeezed until the man went limp and unconscious. Only then did Rostnikov let him down gently to the ground and pause for an instant to be sure the man was still breathing. Karpo, meanwhile, had set down the ladder and stood at the corner of the building, waiting to see if the old guard would show up. According to his calculations, if the old man had not heard the struggle, he would be coming around the corner in five minutes. The old man did not come running. Rostnikov picked up the ladder, and the three men hurried to the fence.

They were in the car and driving away when, through the rear window, Sasha saw the old guard round the corner, spot his fallen fellow, and run toward him. What Sasha did not see was the Chaika parked a quarter of a mile away, a Chaika with its lights out that followed them at a safe distance.

When they were headed back to the center of Moscow, Rostnikov said, "Emil?"

Karpo reached into his jacket and removed three sheets of paper. One sheet was the copy of a typed letter. The other two were copies of delivery orders. Rostnikov took them and joined them with a paper clip to the copies of papers he had made from items in the files of Raya Corspoyva. He would have to look at them carefully, to consider what he had, but even at this point Rostnikov was sure that he held in his hand enough evidence against a ranking KGB member to ensure his own death and that of Karpo and Tkach.

"The guard?" Sasha said.

"I'll deal with that, Sasha," said Rostnikov. "And I will return everything to Petrovka and the badger to the Ferlonika research lab."

"A request, Inspector," Sasha said as they neared his street. "I need a meeting permit for a small group, a public meeting permit. It concerns a lead in the bus case."

"I'll speak to Pankov," said Rostnikov. "Now a question: Where were you tonight?"

"At home, in bed," said Tkach.

"And you, Emil?"

"The same," Karpo said, turning onto the Outer Ring Road.

Rostnikov leaned back, tapping his fingers on the sheaf of papers in his hand, considering his next move.

Within ten minutes of that moment, Sasha had entered his apartment, kissed the sleeping Pulcharia, taken off his clothes, and slid into bed next to Maya, who murmured, "Where were you?"

"Toilet, thinking," he said, realizing that he was very awake and very excited.

Maya's hand reached over languidly to hold him and wandered below his flat belly. In the light they left on in the kitchen alcove, Sasha could see the smile on Maya's face. Her eyes opened dreamily and he pulled her gently to him and kissed her quite deeply.

Within twenty minutes of that moment, Emil Karpo was at the door of his apartment. He checked the thread and hair to be sure no one had entered in his absence, went in, checked the placement of the key objects, and removed his clothes. Emil Karpo always went to sleep instantly upon lying back. He used no pillow and nothing to cover himself.

Before he lay back this night, however, he told himself that he had made an error in visiting the room of Yuri Vostoyavek. There would be no such mistakes in the morning. He reminded himself to awaken in four hours. He could sleep no longer. There was no time.

Within the hour Rostnikov had returned the ladder, the badger, the copying machine, and the automobile; had hidden the papers he had taken from the Lentaka Shoe Factory, and had located a taxi, which was now taking him home. The driver was, fortunately, not a talker. He was sullen, tired, and perhaps just a bit drunk, which was perfectly fine with Porfiry Petrovich, who was also very tired.

———

When the phone rang slightly after two in the morning, the KGB officer picked it up before the echo of the first ring ended. He was expecting the call, had been lying awake in bed. He was alone. His wife had long had her own room, which he could visit when he wished, though it had been some time since he wished or, for that matter, since she had wished him to do so.

"Yes," he said.

"Set," said Vadim. Next to him was the man who had driven the Chaika. Vadim could say no more on the phone, was permitted to say no more. In the morning he would give a full report.

"Good," said the KGB officer and hung up the receiver.

As he lay back, knowing he could not and would not sleep, the KGB officer went over his plan once again and then once more before he decided to move to the kitchen for coffee and the reward of a small piece of Italian chocolate, an indulgence he allowed himself secretly and infrequently, an indulgence he believed he now deserved.

Stuart M. Kaminsky

─────────

It was almost three in the morning when Porfiry Petrovich woke up and reached over to touch Sarah. At first, when he touched the cool, smooth pillow he thought she must be in the washroom or the living room, getting a drink. Sometimes Sarah had difficulty sleeping. She never woke him. Iosef had inherited his mother's occasional sleeplessness. Rostnikov never had trouble sleeping. When his head touched the pillow he was asleep in less than a minute. He could not take naps during the day even when he worked several days without sleep. The nap would only leave him in a weary fog.

When he realized where Sarah was and that he was alone in the apartment, Rostnikov sat up, got out of bed, turned on the light, and looked back at the empty pillows. It was too early to stay up, to read. He thought of his weights, moved into the living room, opened the cabinet in the corner, and pulled out his fifty-pound iron dumbbell. In his pajamas, he sat on a kitchen chair doing curls dreamily, wondering why he was up.

Unfinished business, he thought. And then he let his mind go to silver, a silver he once saw on a door beyond which had been an old man who had told him a terrible secret. The secret had led to a man who had killed seven people.

The sweat would not come. Rostnikov continued.

Perhaps he should read the section in the new book, the section on installing double bends in sink tubing. He imagined copper tubes curling into the bowels of his building, the bowels of the earth, twisting and turning in a pattern that made no sense to him but that some hidden building had concocted to keep Rostnikov forever guessing, forever following the twists and turns he had . . . and then he understood.

Rostnikov was in the middle of the downside of a right-handed curl, his elbow resting on the table. He let the weight down and paid attention while his mind laid out the truth.

Yes, it was so. It explained everything.

He put the dumbbell away carefully, respectfully, closed the cabinet, turned off the light, and went back to the bedroom. He would be able to sleep now.

Chapter Eleven

Yuri Vostoyavek did not tell his mother about the dream of the gaunt man for two reasons. First, he did not wish his mother to know that he had experienced a nightmare and might be seeking her sympathy. Elena Vostoyavek was already too anxious to provide her sympathy to her only son. Second, and perhaps most troubling and important, Yuri was not completely sure that it had been a dream.

It had seemed so tangible, so . . . and then he remembered. He remembered as he put on his shoes and heard the water running in the small bathroom.

"Mother," he called, pausing with one shoe on, "in the night, did you call out to me?"

"Call out? Yes. You knocked over the clock."

"But the clock wasn't on the floor this morning," he said.

Elena turned off the water and came into the combination living room-kitchen-bedroom.

"I picked it up early this morning when you were asleep," she said, looking at him as she adjusted an earring. "What's wrong? Are you ill?"

Yuri stood up quickly, his face pale.

"Wrong? Why are you always asking what is wrong? Nothing is wrong. It's depressing to . . . I'm sorry."

"Does it have to do with . . . ?" she began and then stopped.

"Do with what?" Yuri asked, pausing at the door.

"Do with that girl?" she said softly, hoping he wouldn't be angry, sorry that she had said it.

"I don't know," he said, and left the apartment.

And that answer from her son, that moment of doubt frightened Elena Vostoyavek more than the anger of her son had ever done.

———————

Just before dawn, Porfiry Petrovich had eaten two slices of bread with currant jam and drunk a quart of something called celery-banana juice. He had made his call to Petrovka, asking if there had been any reports of break-ins during the night. He did not explain himself to the clerk. He did not have to. He simply gave his name, rank, and access code.

Then, with the receiver cradled under his ear as he put on his pants, Rostnikov listened to the list of break-ins throughout Moscow. The Lentaka Shoe Factory was fifth on the list, but Rostnikov waited until the clerk had read the full twenty-six. He then requested a full printout on his desk within the hour.

Moments later he had Raya Corspoyva, the party representative at the Lentaka Shoe Factory, on the phone.

"Comrade," he said with concern, "I've just received the morning report and note that an attempted break-in has taken place."

"It was nothing, Inspector," she said. "A mistake."

"It seems strange coming so closely on my visit," he said. "Are you sure this has nothing to do with my inquiries?"

"Nothing," she assured him. "A mistake. Nothing is missing. There is no sign of entry. Had I been here I would have stopped the guard from reporting. I will admit, however, and I hope this does not get into the record, that one of our night security guards got a little drunk and thought he saw someone. Even claimed to have been attacked, though he couldn't identify an attacker."

"Drunk, on duty?" Rostnikov said.

"They have been dismissed," she replied.

"And that is all there is to it?"

"That is all," she said. "You have my word as party member, Comrade."

And, Rostnikov noted, your word does not include the death of a guard dog and the mauling of another.

"Thank you, Comrade," he said. "You have relieved my anxiety."

A few minutes before seven that morning, Sasha Tkach had stood just outside the Arbat Metro station no more than twenty paces from where Emil Karpo had stood the day before when he followed Yuri Vostoyavek. The sun had been bright, the air cool. Though Sasha was tired, he felt as if the world might be considering at least a neutral attitude toward him.

He had begun the morning at six in the Petrovka office checking the computer for licenses issued to flower sellers. There were several Sonias, none of whom was authorized to sell on or near the Arbat.

Yes, the old man could have been lying to him, but Sasha didn't think so. The man wanted the permit to meet, and Sasha, with Rostnikov's help, would deliver it if he found Sonia.

He began making inquiries of vendors and received the description of several flower vendors, though no one knew their names. A one-armed man selling shoelaces in front of a shoestore told him of a girl who might have been named Sonia who usually came to the square around ten to sell flowers. By the time he received this information, it was a few minutes to nine. He bought a copy of *Pravda*, buttoned his jacket, and went back to the square to await the arrival of the flower seller, who might or might not be the Sonia he was seeking.

———

Porfiry Petrovich did not immediately go to Petrovka that morning. In fact, he called in a second time asking to be switched directly to Pankov. He told Pankov that he would be investigating the shoe factory pilfering and would be in sometime in the afternoon to report.

Since Porfiry Petrovich had not once in the several months he had worked for the Gray Wolfhound offered any kind of report to Pankov, the little man was genuinely grateful.

"I will be here and waiting," Pankov said with dignity.

Rostnikov hung up. The copies of documents he had made were in an envelope securely taped to the bottom of the lower right-hand drawer of Pankov's desk. Rostnikov had read them carefully the night before. The link to Nahatchavanski was subtle and circumstantial but evident to a careful observer. Substantial payments had been made to a man named Stylor for "services." Stylor had, in turn, taken this money for unspecified services and turned it over to a fund to establish a memorial for casualties of the Afghan campaign. Gregor Nahatchavanski was the director of this campaign. The documents indicating this link had been clipped together, making it clear that Raya Corspoyva was providing herself with a bit of insurance, a dangerous bit of insurance.

Before he had come home the night before, Rostnikov had used the computer files to verify that Igor Stylor was Gregor Nahatchavanski's brother-in-law and that Igor Stylor was a low-level clerk in the Office of Housing. He also verified that a fund to establish a memorial for Afghan casualties did exist but that to date only a small amount of cash had come in for the fund, which had received very little public attention.

After working out with his weights, taking a quick, cold shower, and dressing, Rostnikov walked to the Metro station and took a train to Sokol Street. One of the items he had found in Lukov's office was the home address on Sokol Street of Ivan Bulgarin.

Rostnikov had no trouble finding the address. It was one of a dozen similar five-story apartment buildings on Sokol. He entered the lobby, ignored the scribbled obscenities on the wall, and searched for the name of Ivan Bulgarin. He did not find it. He did find a door with the name "Mariya Kartonya, Director," written on a gray card. Beyond the door people were arguing loudly. Rostnikov knocked at the door and waited. The argument within continued. Rostnikov knocked again and heard someone come to the door. The door opened and Porfiry Petrovich found himself looking into the face of a small, fat woman in a black dress. The fat woman, who could have been any age from thirty to fifty, had her hands on her hips and did not look pleased to have a visitor.

"What?" she demanded.

Behind her a man shouted. The fat woman turned and screamed at the man to shut up.

"Police," said Rostnikov, showing his card.

"So?" she said.

"I'm looking for Ivan Bulgarin," he said.

"Where are my suspenders?" the man inside the apartment demanded, moving toward the door.

"Who?" the fat woman asked.

"Bulgarin, Ivan," Rostnikov said. "He lives in this building."

"Forget the suspenders," said the man. "I'm leaving."

"No Bulgarin," she said. "Bulgakov, Bulmash. No Bulgarin. Not since I've been here."

"And," said Rostnikov, "how long is that?"

"Twelve years. Twelve years with him," the fat woman said, pointing over her shoulder where the man suddenly appeared. There was nothing to him. He couldn't have weighed more than 120 pounds and couldn't have been younger than sixty-five or seventy.

"Maybe Bulgarin is in one of the other buildings," Rostnikov tried. "A very big man with a beard."

"No," said Mariya, putting up her arm to stop the thin man from escaping past her. "I know the buildings on this street. No Bulgarin. Nobody very big with a beard."

The thin man ducked under the fat woman's arm and dashed past Rostnikov.

"Thank you," said Rostnikov, stepping quickly out of the way to allow her to go in pursuit of her man.

When he arrived at his desk slightly after noon, Rostnikov considered several ways of finding the man who walked like a bear. He was considering this when the phone rang.

Andrei Morchov had risen early this morning, as he did every morning. Now he stood looking at himself in the mirror. He was not completely displeased. He had cultivated a brooding, intense look that had long ago ceased to be a mask. He looked like a man carrying a heavy burden of responsibility, but not just trivial, domestic responsibility. No; Andrei Morchov, as anyone could see who saw him stride quickly to his waiting limousine or put on his glasses to absorb a document, was concerned with matters of great pith and moment. His suits were properly dark. His ties were somber. He never looked as if he needed a shave or haircut. Andrei Morchov knew that he was not a handsome man, but he had presence.

Andrei Morchov adjusted his tie and, in the mirror, saw his daughter Jalna in the next room walking carefully toward the door of the dacha.

"Where are you going?" he said evenly without turning from the mirror. In fact, although he was ready to turn, he continued to watch her reflection. Andrei Morchov knew how to seize and hold an advantage.

"Out, to the city," she said.

"No."

"I have nothing to do here!" she cried.

"Schoolwork. Reading. Gardening."

He pretended to adjust his tie just a bit more.

"I'll go mad here," she said to her father's back. "Mad."

"You'll not go mad," he said, turning.

"I'll leave when you are gone," she said. "You won't even know I've left."

"I'll call from my office," he said, walking past her to get his coat and briefcase at the door.

"I'll say I was in the garden or on the toilet. I'll say I was simply outside loving the trees and grass," she taunted.

"And the flowers," he added.

A smile touched Andrei Morchov's lips, but he controlled it as he adjusted his coat and picked up his briefcase. He could manipulate ministers, confound bureaucrats, and control generals, but it took enormous energy to exert the slightest control over this one teenage girl. There were those in the government who would delight at watching this domestic scene. And it was at this moment that Andrei Morchov realized not for the first time that he truly loved his daughter.

The revelation was quite startling each time it came. They had never gotten along well. Certainly, it had been worse when Mariankaya, the girl's mother, was alive, but it had not improved when she died.

Andrei Morchov stood looking at his daughter. He knew that, like her mother, she was quite beautiful, a pale northern beauty he recognized but that held no intrigue for him. He preferred dark women with the hint of a serpent about them, like Svetlana.

"Why are you looking at me like that?" Jalna asked defiantly. She wore a pair of American jeans and a man's white shirt tied in front the way she had seen it done in a French magazine.

"You'll do as you are told," he said, but he thought as he had on other such occasions that his conflict with his daughter was what kept him truly alive. The rest of his existence was a performance without substance, with any satisfaction long since exhausted. His life, with the exception of this girl, was a chess game he could play with skill and no heat.

"Do you know what?" she said, advancing on him. "Do you know what?" she shouted. "I hate you! I've always hated you!"

And Andrei Morchov did the wrong thing. He laughed. He laughed because she was expressing her hate at a moment in which he was acknowledging to himself a love for her. He laughed because he expected that this rush of affection in him would fade, as it had before, when he was in the backseat of his car looking at the trade union papers. He laughed because the expression of hate in his daughter's eyes was so clearly false. Yes, she hated him, but she hated him because she loved and needed him. She hated him, but she hated herself more for her need of him. And, he realized, even if this feeling of love

195

remained within him, he could and would do nothing about it, as he had done nothing in the past when this feeling for her had come. Their roles were set. He could not simply repent, embrace her, and promise her a new life. They would go on like this till she was grown and moved out or accepted their relationship. The forum of their love would be emotional, volatile. Andrei Morchov had laughed at himself.

The laughter froze Jalna in midstep, and her anger went beyond words.

He was laughing at her, laughing at her. He would not even take her hatred seriously.

"I must go," he said. "I will be home late tonight."

She did not answer. He turned and went out the door, closing it behind him with a firm, controlled snap.

Jalna found herself moving to the window, moving as she had done hundreds, perhaps thousands of times, moving to the window to watch her father pull away in a dark car, pull away and leave her alone for hours, days. She watched the car move slowly down the paved road through the trees. She watched as it turned right and moved out of sight. She watched even when there was no car to see and she decided that when her father returned that night, with or without Yuri, she would kill him.

———————

The flower vendor named Sonia arrived just after ten. Her cart was small, her supply limited to bunches of small yellow flowers. She was, Sasha decided, about twenty and quite pretty if a bit thin. Her dark hair was cut short, and her skin was bronzed by heredity and the sun.

The Man Who Walked Like a Bear

Sasha tucked the newspaper into his pocket and approached as passersby paused to look at the flowers and then generally moved on without buying. As he approached, the girl adjusted the flowers, perking up a bunch in the back with her fingertips, and switching several bunches about.

"Your name is Sonia?" he asked.

She looked up and smiled. Sasha returned the smile.

"Yes," she said.

There was in her voice an accent of the South, not like Maya's Ukrainian accent, which spoke of mountains and the past, but an exotic accent that suggested the Orient.

"Police," he said, removing his wallet and showing his photo identity card.

Before he could put the wallet away she reached over to hold and examine it. A man had been approaching the flower cart, but when he saw Sasha open his wallet and say "Police," he veered away, as if remembering some urgent business elsewhere.

"Sasha," the girl said without fear. "A good name. I had a boyfriend named Sasha once. I stayed with him longer than I should have just because I liked the way our names went together, Sasha and Sonia. It sounds like a balancing act at the circus. You like the circus?"

A bus roared behind them and a wave of shoppers burst from the mouth of the Metro station. Tkach put his wallet away. The girl continued to smile at him.

"You don't seem concerned that I know your name and am a police officer," he said.

"I'm not," she answered.

"That is an attitude I have begun to encounter frequently," he said with a sigh.

"And it disturbs you? You would rather have people afraid of the police?" she asked.

"It would make my life easier," he said.

"But the police, the State exist to serve the people," she said teasingly. "The people are the State."

This was not going at all as Sasha had expected. Instead of investigating a murder he was being given a political lecture by a flower girl in the middle of a busy square. People were passing by, catching snatches of the conversation, and hiding grins. He had to regain control of the situation, though he was not sure he had ever had such control.

"I have some questions I must ask you," he said.

"Here? Now?"

"If not here, where? If not now, when?" he answered, mocking her previous political style.

"Ask," she said, "but ask quickly. I'm losing customers."

Sasha selected a bunch of flowers and handed the girl a kopeck.

"For my wife," he explained.

"In that case," Sonia said, taking the flowers from him and holding out a different bunch, "take the time to give her the freshest ones and not just the first you see."

"Peotor Kotsis," said Sasha, taking the flowers from her and letting his fingers touch her hand so he could feel her response to the name at the same time he watched her expression. He detected nothing. She said nothing.

"You know the name?" he went on, now holding the flowers awkwardly in his hand.

"Yes," she said. "How did you know I—?"

"I must find him," he interrupted.

"Why?"

She busied herself readjusting the flowers to cover the space left by Sasha's purchase.

"We have reason to suspect that he may be involved in a major crime," said Sasha. "That is all I can tell you. What can you tell me?"

"Peotor Kotsis is from the same town in Turkistan that my family is from," Sonia said, still smiling but a smile that had lost its mirth. "The Kotsis family long before it was fashionable grumbled about independence. People in our town were afraid of him, his son, the whole family. People in our town humored Kotsis and were relieved when he and his brood left the town. Kotsis vowed to come back a liberator and a hero who had brought independence to Turkistan, to come back a hero or die a martyr."

"And he came to Moscow?" Sasha prodded, shifting his flowers once more, sorry he had purchased them. A fat woman jostled Sasha, who immediately felt for his wallet and found it still there.

"First through the South, town to town, village to village, locating Turkistanis, recruiting their support, intimidating them into giving him and his growing band food and shelter," Sonia said, looking beyond Sasha toward the South, though the view was blocked by a massive building.

"And you were with him?" Sasha asked.

"I was with them," she said, nodding. "I convinced myself that I believed in the Turkistani liberation. I convinced myself because I wanted to get out of that long-dead town of decaying wood and forgotten memories. I was a young girl, and these people were wild and exciting."

"You are still a young girl," Sasha said.

199

"A young woman," Sonia corrected, pointing a mock scolding finger at him.

"Do you know where Peotor Kotsis is?"

"You mean where he is right now?" she asked in return.

"Now, soon, whatever," said Sasha.

"Come back here at noon," she said. "I'll take you home. You can talk to my father. He'll know where Peotor Kotsis is. He'll know where his son Vasily is. He'll know whatever you need to know. Whether he will tell you is between you and him."

"Noon," he said.

She waved as he walked away, and Sasha nodded back. He wasn't sure what he would do with the flowers. There wasn't time to take them home for Maya, and he had things to do before he returned to the square to meet Sonia at noon.

And then he got a wonderful idea. Lydia, his mother, worked only a few minutes from here. He found a phone, made his call, and then walked up the street to the Office of Information. He identified himself to the guard at the desk and went up the elevator to the floor where Lydia worked. Although she had worked there for almost two decades, Sasha had entered the building only four times, and one of those was in conjunction with the investigation of a series of murders along the Moscow River. The murderer had never been caught.

On the sixth floor, Sasha located his mother's supervisor, who politely told the policeman that he could certainly talk to Lydia for a few minutes. The supervisor, who was no older than Sasha, looked at the flowers without comment.

Lydia was seated at her desk in a corner away from the

other workers in her section. She did not hear her son approach. But Lydia Tkach heard very little in any case.

"Mother," Sasha announced.

She didn't respond. He stepped in front of her into her field of vision and she looked up.

She was a small woman in a no-nonsense business suit, her gray straight hair tied back with a dark band that matched the color of her suit. Once, Sasha thought, she had been a beauty. The cheekbones were still there. The eyes were still bright.

"Who died?" Lydia shouted. "Maya? The baby? Uncle Mikhail?"

"No one died," Sasha said, looking around as the woman at a nearby desk looked at him. "I was nearby and wanted to bring you this."

He reached down with the flowers and her hand came up to take them and then pulled back, as if sensing a trap within the bright petals.

"What is this?" she demanded.

"Flowers, Mother," he said. "Just flowers. I was in—"

"Bribes," she said, looking around the room toward her fellow workers, who did their best to ignore her. "My own son is reduced to bribes with wilting flowers. I can't be bought, Sasha. I cannot be bought. You want to throw me into the street. That you can do, but you cannot salve your conscience with a few flowers."

"Mother, this is—"

"I don't even like this kind of flower," she said in exasperation. "You've known me thirty years and you don't know what kind of flowers I like."

"I'm only twenty-nine, Mother, and I thought you liked all flowers. You always say you—"

She reached over, took the flowers from him, and gave him a look of deep contempt.

"That baby needs me," she said, fishing into a drawer for a glass, which she popped onto the desk and filled with the flowers. "You don't just take a baby from her grandmother."

"No one is taking . . . Mother, we've been through all this."

"*You've* been through all this," she said. "*I* listened. *You* talked."

It was clear to Sasha that everyone within five or six miles was listening to his mother shout. They had no choice even if they had no interest.

"I've got to get back to work, Mother," he said.

His mother glared up at him. Sasha leaned over the desk and kissed her head.

"The flowers aren't so bad," she said.

"Thank you."

"You doing something dangerous today?" she asked, her voice dropping several decibels as she looked up at him.

"What makes you—?" he began.

"Porfiry Petrovich," she said loudly. "Chief Inspector Rostnikov took me to lunch yesterday and told me about you. Are you doing anything dangerous?"

"No," he lied. "Inspector Rostnikov . . . ?"

"Take care of yourself," she said, looking down at her work and ending the conversation.

"You, too," he said, taking a step back.

"Of course. Who will if I don't?"

With that Sasha made his escape, vowing never again to visit his mother at work.

He made it back to the square a few minutes before noon and found that Sonia had sold most of her flowers.

She smiled up at him. Her teeth, he noticed, were remarkably white and even.

"You brought your flowers home?" she asked, pushing her cart toward him. "How did your wife like them?"

"I gave them to my mother," he said, falling into step beside her.

"You want another bunch for your wife?" Sonia asked.

"Perhaps, after I see your father," he said.

"Is your wife pretty?" Sonia asked, maneuvering her cart down a curb.

"Yes," he said.

"Of course," Sonia said with a laugh, dodging behind a car, the wheels of the cart clattering. "A pretty policeman would have a pretty wife. Nothing else would make sense."

"You're sure your father will be home?" he asked.

"He'll be home," she said. "But he'll be leaving for work soon. Maybe you and I can talk a bit then. I can tell you more about Kotsis. And other things. Sasha and Sonia."

She moved quickly, and he had to hurry to keep up with her.

"Is it far?" he asked.

A barrel of a man stepped back awkwardly to avoid the momentum of the flower cart.

"Not far," she said. "Right down this way."

"Can we move a bit slower?" Sasha said. "I don't want to arrest you for dangerous driving."

Sonia slowed down.

"Better?" she asked.

"Better," he said.

She took his arm and pushed the cart expertly with one hand. Sasha did not pull away.

"Right over there," she said, pointing to a small, slightly run-down ancient building that had managed to escape

203

the demolition and rebuilding of the 1950s. She opened the door with a key and maneuvered the cart through expertly, though it looked to Sasha as if there was no room to do so. There was almost no light in the alcove in which Sasha found himself. He could barely see the outline of the flower cart as Sonia pushed it into a corner.

"This way," she said, taking his hand and pushing open a door.

Her hand was warm and rough and not at all unpleasant.

There was a bit more light on the stairway she led him up. A solitary small and dirty window on the landing above them allowed them to see the worn-down wooden stairs. On the second floor, Sonia tugged him to the left.

"Right here," she said. She let go of his hand, inserted her key in the lock, and opened the door.

Sasha stepped into the small room behind her. There were a few pieces of old furniture, a worn sofa, a table with three chairs, a lamp, and a dresser with a radio atop it. A small rug hid few of the stains on the dirty floor. Sonia closed the door and called out, "Father, we're here!"

A man came through the door to the right, a somber man in dark pants, a flannel shirt, and a blue jacket. In his right hand he held a pistol, which he aimed directly at Sasha Tkach's chest.

"This is my father, Sasha," Sonia said. "Peotor Kotsis."

Chapter Twelve

Emil Karpo had six officially active cases to deal with. He also had 604 officially inactive cases to deal with. The 604 cases on which he kept records in black notebooks on the shelves in his small room were those that had been placed in the inactive files of the Procurator's Office and the MVD. Only twenty-three of these cases had been assigned originally to Karpo. In the past fourteen years Emil Karpo had brought sixteen of those cases to satisfactory conclusions either by apprehending the lawbreaker or by discovering that those responsible were dead or had left the country.

Emil Karpo's evenings were spent updating his records of those cases and conducting his investigations. His holidays were spent following leads, sometimes leads on cases fifteen or twenty years old. The oldest case in Emil Karpo's file involved the murder of a doctor on the Fili Metro platform twenty-nine years earlier.

Of the current cases to which he had been assigned, he was most confident that he could and would locate those responsible for kidnapping pets, particularly cats in the housing complexes near the airport. He was making a slow, deliberate investigation of both government-authorized and black market sausage and ground-meat distributors. The operation was too big and too much in need of distributors to keep quiet. The crimes that were most difficult to deal with were those that involved apparently random acts of violence by individuals against others they did not know. When the perpetrator simply acted once and receded and no witnesses were present, it was almost impossible to deal with. Like the person who killed the doctor on the Metro platform. Almost impossible.

What Karpo really wanted to do was deal with Yuri Vostoyavek and Jalna Morchov, and he would have done so if he knew where the boy was. Karpo had waited for Yuri outside the apartment where he lived, but the boy had not come out. His mother had emerged around eight, hurrying to catch a bus, but by nine Yuri was not down. Perhaps he had been too frightened by Karpo to get up and go to work. This Karpo doubted. Karpo had, in fact, admired the boy's reaction to his intrusion.

A few minutes after nine, Karpo had climbed the stairs and knocked at the door to the Vostoyavek apartment. There was no answer. He had used his identity card to open the door and found the apartment empty. The conclusion was simple: Expecting to be followed, the boy had gotten out through an alternate exit.

After concluding that Yuri had not gone to work, Karpo had gone to his desk at Petrovka and called the dacha of Andrei Morchov. The girl, Jalna, answered the phone. Her "Yes, who is it?" had held a challenge.

"Comrade Morchov, please," he said.

"He just left," she said.

"Thank you," he said and hung up.

The next step was obvious: Karpo rose, signed out on the board near the sixth-floor exit, and went out in search of Andrei Morchov.

═══════

"Policeman," Peotor Kotsis said, shaking his head, "you are an annoyance."

Sonia moved behind Sasha and quickly, efficiently searched him, finding his pistol and pulling it out with a satisfied, "Uh."

She displayed it to her father, who nodded his approval and pointed to the table. Sonia bounced over and placed the weapon gently next to a steaming cup of liquid.

"Sit, policeman," Kotsis said, pointing to the sofa with his gun. Sasha moved to the sofa and sat.

Sonia sat at the table, put her finger in the barrel of Sasha's gun, and spun it gently as she sipped the hot liquid.

"Sonia and Sasha," she said with a smile, and Sasha concluded that the lovely young woman was more than a bit mad.

"The old man," Sasha said.

"Yes," agreed Kotsis. "The old man. The woman at the center. You have, as others before you have done for two centuries, underestimated the determination of the Turkistani. You have been, as the Americans used to say and the French continue to say in their pale imitations of old movies, set up."

"Why?" asked Sasha.

"Hostage," said Sonia.

"Yes," agreed Peotor. "We plan to take a series of hostages. We've learned much from the mistakes in Lebanon. You are, in fact, the second of our hostages. We have no illusions about your value to the government. Therefore, we will make your kidnapping public knowledge. We will make our reasons quite public. We will make the citizens of Moscow, of the Soviet Union, afraid to walk in the streets. We will make them so afraid that the government will give us independence. Oh, they won't say that our actions are the reason. They'll say it is part of the massive reform. They will give it with other concessions in other areas, but it will be because of us. It will take time, but they will be worn down."

"You're not going to kill me?" asked Sasha.

"No," said Peotor. "Not yet, not unless we have to. Are you disappointed?"

"No," said Sasha.

"We can be friends," said Sonia, happily turning the barrel of the pistol in Sasha's direction.

"You're going to keep me here?" Sasha asked.

"No," said Kotsis. "You are going to put out your hands in a few minutes so that Sonia can put handcuffs on you. Then we will go to a car and take you someplace out of town."

"Where?" asked Sasha.

"Why is it that you don't seem particularly surprised by all this?" said Peotor Kotsis, looking a bit puzzled. "A bit frightened, yes. I've learned to recognize that, but not surprised."

Sasha was about to answer when the door through

which he and Sonia had come burst off its hinges and skidded across the floor. Kotsis turned his gun toward the sound, but two quick shots from the doorway tore into his chest. The gun in Kotsis's hand flew across the room and hit the wall. A spray of bullets spat out, thudding into the wall.

Sasha was on the floor now, his eyes on Sonia, who watched her father slump to the floor. She turned, her hand still clutching the cup of hot liquid, and faced the figure in the doorway who had shot her father. Her hand reached for Sasha's gun.

"No!" Sasha cried.

Zelach stood in the doorway, his pistol leveled at the girl, but he hesitated. In the instant between time, Sonia smiled at Sasha, lifted his pistol to her mouth, pulled the trigger, and blew off the top of her head.

"God!" Sasha screamed.

Zelach stepped into the room, his pistol leveled at the fallen Peotor Kotsis. "Dead," he said.

Porfiry Petrovich stepped through the doorway and looked at Sasha, who sat shaking on the floor. Rostnikov put an arm around the younger man and helped him to his feet.

"I can't do this anymore," Tkach said.

"I know," said Rostnikov.

Tkach's eyes were wide and focused on the mutilated body of the girl who moments before had been smiling.

"You were late," Tkach said, trembling, near breakdown.

"You moved quickly," said Rostnikov. "I do not move so quickly."

"I mean it, Porfiry Petrovich," he said as Zelach turned

and Rostnikov nodded to him. Zelach left the room in search of a phone.

"You mean it now," said Rostnikov. "I have meant it each time. You did very well."

"Very well?" said Sasha, looking more than a bit wild, his hair dangling over his eyes. "They're dead."

"And you are alive, Sasha," said Rostnikov. "We'll talk more of this later. Now I need your help. There is still a bus and a driver to find, and more people will die if we do not find them. You understand, Sasha, when the others discover what has happened here, they will probably want to do something very violent. We must find them, Sasha. You and I. We must find them."

"Yes," said Sasha, panting. "We must find them."

"We must search these rooms quickly, Sasha," he said. "Zelach is calling this in. The KGB will be involved. We must search these rooms and find something to lead us to the rest of these people."

Sasha nodded his head, stood up straight, and brushed back his hair.

"Then let's do it," he said.

Too many variables. That is what the KGB officer thought as he paced his room. Too many variables. The knock came and he moved to his desk, sat, composed himself, folded his hands, and told the man at the door to enter.

The man came in, closed the door behind him, and moved in front of the desk.

"Sit," said the KGB officer.

"You know about the call?" Vadim said, sitting. He had never before been invited to sit in this office. He took it as a bad sign.

"Variables," said the KGB officer.

"Variables, yes," said Vadim. He didn't like what was going on here, didn't like it at all. The officer was always composed, superior. There were signs here of concern, and if the officer was concerned, Vadim had reason to be concerned, too.

"Go on," said the officer.

"Both Rostnikov and Tkach are devoting full attention to what now appears to be a terrorist situation," Vadim said. "I would assume Rostnikov will pull the other one, Karpo, from his case to join them. The investigative bureau has officially been brought in and is taking over the situation. It is now a KGB operation, but . . ."

". . . but that will not stop Rostnikov," the officer said.

Vadim shrugged.

"It is in our best interest to conclude the situation as soon as possible," he said.

"Find the terrorists. Finish them. Our plan requires that this be concluded quickly. Every minute, every hour this goes on we run the risk of being discovered," the KGB man said.

Vadim nodded in agreement.

———

Emil Karpo concluded before noon that Andrei Morchov was safely inside the walls of the Kremlin and would be there till at least seven that night for meetings. This much he had learned directly from Morchov's secretary after identifying himself.

He called in to Petrovka to let the duty officer know he was proceeding to another investigation. Rostnikov, calling Petrovka seconds later, missed him, but left a message.

Karpo spent most of the afternoon tracking down informants and getting a line on a meat dealer who seemed to be a promising lead, not necessarily because he would be the one dealing in the meat of dead cats and dogs but that he would be likely to know who was doing so. Karpo checked his notebook and at a few minutes after three decided, since he was not far from Dynamo Stadium, to interview a ticket saleswoman who had witnessed an armed robbery two years earlier. He had interviewed her six months ago, but there were a few variations on earlier questions he wished to try.

By five, Emil Karpo was sitting at his desk in his apartment, carefully copying the notes he had taken into the properly filed black notebooks on the shelves that lined his room.

The knock on his door was firm and confident. If Karpo were given to or capable of smiling, he would be smiling now as he rose, moved a few feet across the room, and opened the door to Yuri Vostoyavek.

"Come in," he said, and the boy entered.

"I've been following you," Yuri said aggressively.

"I know," said Karpo. "There is only one chair. You may sit."

"I don't want to sit," Yuri said, facing Karpo.

"You are not tired?"

"Of course I'm tired," the boy said. "You've been running me all over the city for hours."

"You did well," said Karpo. "I didn't pick you up till I left my office."

They were facing each other as they had the previous night in Yuri's room.

"You have something to tell me?" asked Karpo.

"I'd like to beat the hell out of you," said the boy.

"A natural reaction," said Karpo. "But beyond that?"

"You are a policeman," said Yuri.

"I am aware of that," said Karpo.

"I'm not afraid of you," said Yuri.

"You're not?"

"Well, I am, but it makes no difference. That's not why I'm going to say this," Yuri said. "I've given up . . . what I was considering. You understand?"

"I understand," said Karpo.

"But . . . I can't stop Jalna. She plans to . . . I think she might . . . She has my gun . . . tonight. When he gets back to the dacha. She said . . . I can't get out there. They stop me when I try."

"Then," said Karpo, "I suggest we go together."

It was a bit after six. If they hurried, Karpo could get a car on an emergency requisition and they could get to Morchov's dacha by seven-thirty if they rode the center lane all the way.

———

By six, when Peotor had not returned, Vasily and the girl Lia went to the nearby village to call Sonia. They left the three others with Boris Trush, who was ordered to ready his bus for action "very soon."

215

Boris, in fact, knew almost nothing about the mechanics of buses, automobiles, or bicycles, but he went to work in the dark barn fiddling with tools, calling for wrenches, and working himself into a sweat, which he hoped would convince his captors of both his zeal and his ability.

Vasily and Lia found a phone in a small all-purpose grocery that sold Coca-Cola. The old woman who ran the store eyed them suspiciously but backed off when Vasily asked her pointedly what she was looking at and offered to show her much more if she was really interested.

Sonia's phone rang eight times before someone picked it up.

"Sonia?" Vasily said.

A long pause and a woman's voice,

"She's not in. She had to go out to pick up some flowers for tomorrow."

"Who are you?" Vasily demanded.

"Mrs. Barakov, across the hall. Wait, I think I hear her coming in downstairs."

The line went silent as Vasily waited, shifted his weight from one foot to the other, and drained what was left of his Coke.

"Hello!" he shouted after ten seconds. "Where the hell . . ."

And then it dawned on him. He looked at the phone, let out a yowl of pain that made Lia turn to him from a stack of canned fruit she was examining, and brought a frightened gasp from the old woman who ran the little store.

Vasily hung up the phone and turned to Lia.

"Let's go," he said.

"I just—" she began but he didn't let her finish. He pushed her toward the door.

At the door, Vasily turned to the trembling woman behind the counter.

"Old woman," he said, "in a few minutes men will be here looking for us. You tell them I am a tall, dark, and fat man. You do not tell them about her. You tell them any more and I will be back to rip out your nostrils and scream into your skull."

Outside, Vasily looked one way and then the other.

"What's going on?" Lia asked.

"They got Sonia. They probably got my father." Vasily was crying with rage. He stamped his foot on the ground. "I let them have time to trace the call. We have to hurry. We have to hurry. We have to do it now. Tonight."

———————

The drive to Morchov's dacha in Zhukovka took Karpo and Yuri thirty minutes. Karpo drove down Kalinin Prospekt, turned left at the arch commemorating the defeat of Napoleon, and displayed the pass that allowed them to drive in the fast lane of the highway. They said nothing as they passed row after row of housing developments, developments that looked just a bit cleaner as they moved farther away from the city. Twenty minutes from the time they left the center of Moscow, they were in the middle of a forest. Police sentry boxes came more frequently now, and many of the license plates began with GAL and ended with four letters, signaling to citizens that the KGB were inside each vehicle watching,

217

protecting the nearby elite. Karpo knew that these men were not here to remain hidden. They were here to warn off those who were not welcome, the curious and the unwary travelers.

Karpo was stopped once on the way to Morchov's dacha. He identified himself to the KGB man just at the turnoff to the dacha and said that he had an appointment with the representative.

"We weren't informed," the man said.

"I suggest you call Comrade Morchov to confirm," said Karpo. "He may simply have had other things on his mind."

The KGB man checked his identification, glanced suspiciously at Yuri, and motioned for them to pass. There was no car on the path in front of the wooden house. Karpo parked and got out. Yuri did the same, and they walked to the front door.

Karpo knocked. There was no answer. He knocked again. No answer. He tried the door, and it opened.

Once inside they heard a voice, a deep, even voice. The policeman and the boy moved toward the voice, through the doorway, and into a large, bright room with modern Scandinavian furniture. Sitting in one chair was Jalna Morchov, a gun in her hand. Across from her sat Andrei Morchov.

Morchov looked up at the intruders. His expression revealed nothing.

"You are not welcome here," he said. "You will turn around and leave immediately."

Karpo and Yuri stopped in the doorway.

"No!" cried Jalna. "No more orders. You can't give orders. You are a dead man. Dead men don't give orders."

"Jalna," Morchov said reasonably, "if you were going to do it, you would have done it by now."

In response, Jalna fired. The bullet ruined Andrei Morchov's new suit as it entered just below his right shoulder. Morchov jerked back in pain, bit his lower lip, and then sat upright again.

"I was wrong," Morchov said. He turned to Karpo and Yuri. "You might as well sit down." Then to Jalna. "If you plan to shoot me again, I would appreciate your giving me some notice. I do not like surprises."

Jalna held the pistol tightly, still aimed in the general direction of her father. Though he was the one who had been shot, she was the one who seemed to be in shock.

"Jalna," Yuri said.

"I've got to do it now," she said.

"No," said Yuri.

"I think she's right," said Morchov.

"We can't," Yuri said.

"Perhaps we can reach some manner of compromise," Karpo suggested.

"I don't see how," said Morchov. "What options have I? You know the law, Comrade. A member of the Politburo has just been intentionally shot."

"She's your daughter," Yuri said.

"Inspector, is that a legal consideration?" Morchov asked, wincing. The blood was pulsing from the wound.

"No," said Karpo.

"Do you believe in circumventing the law, Comrade?" Morchov asked.

"Stop it!" screamed Jalna. "You are always so sure, so reasonable. Aren't you in pain? Aren't you worried about dying?"

"I have lived by reason and argument," Morchov said reasonably. "I see no reason because death is facing me to abandon what I have lived by. You understand me, don't you, Inspector?"

"I understand," said Karpo.

He stepped forward and held his hand out to Jalna. She hesitated for only an instant and then handed the weapon to the policeman.

Yuri moved quickly to the weeping girl and took her in his arms. Morchov sat watching.

"Where is the phone?" Karpo asked.

"In the room you came through," answered Morchov. "Near the door to the bedroom on the left. There is a medical unit in town no more than ten minutes away."

Karpo moved quickly, found the phone, and called for an ambulance before moving back into the bright dining room. No one spoke. No one had anything to say. Karpo found a clean towel and attempted to stop the bleeding. The wound was certainly painful if not serious, at least not serious if the bleeding was soon stopped.

The ambulance arrived within five minutes. Karpo handed the gun to Morchov and went to the door to let the driver and accompanying doctor in. Behind them were the two KGB men who had stopped Karpo and Yuri on the road outside.

"Where?" the doctor, a thin, nervous woman said.

Karpo led her and the driver into the room where Morchov lay. In the corner, Jalna and Yuri stood watching, waiting.

"What happened?" the KGB man asked.

The driver and doctor were helping Morchov to his feet.

"I . . ." Jalna began.

"I shot myself," Morchov said. "I was putting my pistol away and it went off. I'd prefer to keep this as quiet as possible. I have a cabinet meeting in two days."

The KGB man said nothing but continued to eye Karpo with suspicion.

Karpo moved with the nurse and driver toward the door while the KGB men stepped toward Jalna and Yuri to question them.

"I can do without a scandal," Morchov said.

"And that is the only reason," asked Karpo.

"What other reason might there be?" asked Morchov.

"He must be left alone," the doctor said. "He's lost quite a bit of blood."

"I would like my daughter and her friend to accompany me if they wish," Morchov said, looking at the two KGB men huddled over his daughter and Yuri. Jalna's eyes met her father's.

"Yes," she said.

The KGB men hesitated for an instant, and Karpo stepped back to let the boy and girl pass.

Chapter Thirteen

Less than six minutes after Vasily Kotsis hung up the receiver in the small grocery beyond the Outer Ring, the first car containing KGB men arrived. There were two men inside, both in dark blue suits, both quite solemn, and both carrying weapons when they stepped out.

The old woman watching from the window was named Bella Vitz. Because her ankles were always swollen, Bella spent most of her days in the window of the store. Her customers, all local farmers and the people who worked for farmers, took their merchandise, brought it to her, and she collected. Bella was known throughout the community as the Queen of England because she claimed to be related to the British royal family in some strange way she would gladly relate.

"I'm a loyal Soviet citizen," she would begin. "And I'm ashamed to admit this, but I am a second cousin to the British Queen Elizabeth."

As a member of a royal family, Bella had lofty opinions on many matters. At the moment, watching the armed men get out of the car and approach her shop, Bella had opinions about weapons. Everyone seemed to have a gun now. People were shooting people like American cowboys. She heard about it, even read about it with greater frequency in *Pravda*. That crazy young man who threatened her. He had a gun. These men, obviously KGB, had guns. She knew five farmers within six miles who had guns.

The two KGB men with the guns came through the doorway carefully, like in a movie Bella saw years ago. The first one had his gun high, in two hands. The second one crouched low. One aimed his gun to the left. The other to the right.

"He's gone," said Bella, sitting as erect as she could upon her high-backed chair and pulling her sweater around her.

The two men stepped in cautiously, and the shorter of the two spoke.

"The person who made the phone call?" he asked.

"Gone. There was a girl with him. Chinese. Tatar. Who knows?" said Bella.

"Where did they go?"

Now the men were inside, and another car was arriving outside. There were five men in this one. Three of them, she could see when they got out, were in uniform. All of them were carrying weapons.

"He said he would tear off my ear and eat my brain if I told you," she said. "He was just trying to frighten me. People like that don't have time to go back and kill everyone they meet."

The five new men rushed in now with guns waving. One of the new ones not wearing a uniform stepped forward, and the man who had been talking to Bella moved off.

"Where is he?" the new man said.

"They," she corrected. "A young man and a girl. The young man's name is Vasily. I heard the girl call him that. He had bushy yellow hair and crazy eyes and was wearing American jeans and a gray jacket made out of . . . who knows?"

Bella watched all the men scrambling around her store and outside. She wondered if any of them would buy anything.

"Where are they?"

"Who knows?" said Bella. "I've got some thoughts."

"Share them," said the new KGB man, who had a rather large Rumanian-looking nose.

"I'm a loyal citizen of the Soviet Union," she said. "And I am ashamed to admit it, but I am second cousin to the Queen of England."

"What did she look like?" the man asked as the first duo who had entered Bella's shop returned and gave the new leader a negative nod.

And more KGB men arrived. A small truck screeched up in front of the store with eight armed and uniformed men in back. They jumped out.

"She has a round German face. Very sad, very dignified," said Bella. "People say there is a resemblance."

"Not the Queen of England," the man said. "The girl who was with the young man who made the phone call."

"Chinese," said Bella with a sigh. "They said they would fry my intestines and give my liver to the crows if I told about them."

"You are a loyal citizen, Comrade . . ."

"Vitz," she said. "Yes, I am loyal, as was my husband, who worked as a gardener for four years once on a dacha owned by one of Brezhnev's deputies. I am loyal but I am, unfortunately, tainted with royal blood."

The store was swarming with clomping, nodding men with guns. Some were at the phone in the back; others were climbing the steps to her room. Some were still outside. And yet a new leader emerged to stand next to the man with the nose who had been talking to Bella.

"You said you have some thoughts," the KGB man with the nose said.

"Too many guns," said Bella, nodding her head wisely. "In England, the police do not have guns."

"They do now," the latest KGB man corrected her.

"Terrible," said Bella.

"Do you have any thoughts about where this Vasily and the girl might be?" the KGB man with the nose said with infinite patience.

"Yes," said Bella, watching one of the young uniformed men fingering a box of crackers.

"Would you share that information with us?"

"The old Chustoy farm," said Bella. "Three miles north on this road, turn right just past a broken tree, and it's a few hundred yards. Siminov, who has a farm not far from there, saw a city bus drive into the Chustoy place on Monday. That's where I think they are."

The KGB man in charge shouted an order, and seconds later the store and the driveway in front of it were empty. They had purchased nothing, not even thanked her.

The world, Bella thought, is getting to be a very strange and dangerous place. Perhaps she should buy a gun.

The KGB had been just as efficient earlier that morning when Zelach called following the incident in Sonia Kotsis's rooms. Rostnikov, Tkach, and Zelach had all explained what had taken place to the investigator in charge.

"And," the man questioning them had said, "you believed this was all about a missing bus driver?"

"Who," Rostnikov said, "had gotten drunk and stolen his bus."

"And the girl was . . . ?" the man probed.

"Someone told me she knew the driver," said Tkach.

The KGB man smiled and shook his head in disbelief.

"I know you, Rostnikov," he said. "You've stepped on too many tails. Why did you come here with guns if you thought this was just about a drunken bus driver?"

"We expected no trouble," Rostnikov explained.

"No trouble," Zelach added a bit too emphatically.

"I arrived first," said Tkach. "And was surprised to hear the woman, Sonia Kotsis, confess that this case involved terrorist activity. I had asked Inspector Rostnikov to join me here. He came. She opened the door, and this man came out with a gun."

"Officer Zelach responded instinctively and saved our lives," said Rostnikov.

"Rostnikov," the KGB man said, leaning forward, "you are stepping on tails again. Who is going to believe this story?"

"I've kept Colonel Snitkonoy informed about every step of this investigation," Rostnikov said. "And I plan to report to him directly after leaving here."

229

The KGB man sighed and told the three policemen to put their reports in writing, to make no copies, and to hand-deliver the originals to KGB headquarters at Lubyanka as soon as possible. They were then dismissed.

On the way down the stairs from the apartment, Tkach stopped.

"The flowers will die," he said. "We should do something."

"They will die in any case," said Rostnikov.

"Porfiry Petrovich," Tkach said softly, "I can't stand thinking of them slowly dying in that cart, in that dark corner."

"Zelach, you like flowers?" asked Rostnikov.

"I don't know," said Zelach as they reached the bottom of the dark stairway leading down from Sonia's rooms.

"You are not a romantic, Zelach. You shoot well, but you are not a romantic," said Rostnikov, stepping over to pull the flower cart out of shadows.

"I'd rather shoot well," said Zelach.

"Take flowers to your mother, Zelach," Rostnikov said, handing a bunch to the policeman.

Tkach looked at the last six clusters of flowers on the cart.

"Let's give them away," Tkach suggested.

"By all means," Rostnikov agreed, reaching over to scoop up bunches of flowers and handing them to Zelach, who took them awkwardly. Then he turned to Sasha Tkach and whispered, "You did well upstairs, Sasha. Don't go insane on me. We have enough madmen in this country. We need more sane ones who worry about flowers."

"I'll be all right," Tkach said, stepping over to the cart and looking down at it. A sheet of paper was taped to the inside of the cart, not hidden but not exposed either.

Tkach picked it up, looked at it, and handed it to Rostnikov. On the paper was a list, apparently a list of things Sonia would have done that day had she lived to do them. The list read:

> *Market, Cheese Father Likes, any juice*
> *Flower seller, try the Italian at five*
> *Check distance to entrance to tomb, close enough?*
> *Wash the yellow sweater*

Rostnikov looked at Tkach.
"Inspector, the flowers are dripping on me," said Zelach.
Rostnikov folded the note and put it into his pocket.
"Then," he said, "let's take them out into the sun."

When Karpo returned to Petrovka and moved to his desk, he found a bunch of flowers in a drinking glass in the corner. He looked around the office to see whose joke this might be and saw Rostnikov waving at him from beyond the glass window to his office. Karpo moved between the desks, past a woman in uniform carrying a stack of files, and into Rostnikov's office, where the inspector sat, pen in hand, drawing something on the pad before him. Next to the pad was a bunch of flowers just like those on Karpo's desk.
"You like the flowers, Emil Karpo?"
"I neither like nor dislike flowers, Comrade," he said. "I understand their ritual, symbolic function for State events but find nothing personal to respond to. The time

it takes to purchase and place them is time better spent on productive tasks."

"I gather you have just thanked me for giving the flowers to you," said Rostnikov. "Enough of flowers. Morchov. I returned and found a note from the colonel to report at three on the investigation and condition of Andrei Morchov. It is ten minutes to that hour."

Karpo gave his report while standing, and Rostnikov ceased his drawing to listen, nod, and ask a few questions.

"And," Karpo concluded, "I believe I should be given an official reprimand or dismissal for my improper conduct of this investigation."

"You like the boy," Rostnikov said, standing with both hands on the desk. His left leg had given him the warning that if he did not attend to it, it would punish him.

"It would seem so," said Karpo. "And I allowed that response, which I do not understand, to interfere with my performance of duty. I should have acted more decisively. Had I done so, Comrade Morchov, a valued member of the Politburo, would not have been at risk, would not have been shot."

"But he is alive and will be well, Emil Karpo. And no one is going to Lubyanka," said Rostnikov. "What troubles you, Emil?"

"Emotion has no place in an investigation," he said without emotion.

"For me it is everything in an investigation," said Rostnikov.

"Not for me," replied Karpo. "I cannot carry on the scope of my mission, my responsibility if my judgment is clouded by personal response. We are quite different people, Inspector."

"So I have noticed, Emil Karpo," said Rostnikov with a sigh. "So I have noticed. You are not reprimanded. You are not dismissed. I need you. But first look at this."

Rostnikov turned the pad of paper upon which he had been drawing so that Karpo could see the elaborate tangle of curved and intertwined parallel lines.

"Do you know what that is, Emil Karpo?"

"No, I do not," Karpo said, looking at the pad.

"That is the water pipe system in my apartment building," said Rostnikov with satisfaction. "The light paths are the incoming pipelines and the shadowed ones the outgoing. A building can be seen as a replica of the human body. It has a furnace, which is the heart of the body, and a vascular system of pipes to distribute the heat."

"Interesting," said Karpo without interest.

"I have a point, Emil," Rostnikov said, pausing to check his watch. "It is not a coincidence that this metaphor exists, that buildings, institutions can be seen as replicas of the human body. Man makes the world in his own image. He believes the most efficient way for things to work is the way that he works. Are you following me?"

"Yes, Inspector, but not anticipating where we are going."

"I'm fascinated by plumbing, Emil Karpo," said Rostnikov. "I fancy when I repair it that I am a surgeon, a specialist, and the building is my patient. And I gain satisfaction from this because I know that the system can be reduced to a complex drawing and that once the source of a problem is located it can be repaired. That is quite different from the way we work, Emil. Each suspect, each victim, each witness we meet is more than a predictable series of pipes and heating systems. People are confusion and contradiction. You can tell yourself that you are a logical system, Emil. You can suppress emotion and contradiction but you can't overcome them. Sometimes it is better to accept the random emotion and its consequences. Do you now understand why I am telling you this?"

Rostnikov moved from behind his desk and picked up the small bouquet of flowers.

"I believe so, Comrade," said Karpo. "You see no function in my exploring the reasons why I responded to Yuri Vostovayek. I believe I can accept that. You also have some task to perform that you would prefer to avoid. You told me all of this at some length, when a few words would suffice, to forestall the moment when you would have to deal with this task. I would say the task involves talking to the colonel and a subject you are not looking forward to addressing and that has nothing to do with what has happened to Comrade Morchov."

Rostnikov laughed.

"Correct, Emil," he said. "And you came to that conclusion from your knowledge of my past behavior and the nature of my conversation."

"Observation and logic," said Karpo.

"Some might call it intuition," said Rostnikov, smelling the flowers. "Zelach and Tkach are in Red Square. You'll find them in the vicinity of Lenin's Tomb. Please join them. Sasha will explain."

And with that, Rostnikov took his flowers and departed.

There had been no time to think. Boris Trush had been pretending to work on the bus when Vasily and the girl Lia had returned. Boris had been ordered to put on his uniform and get the bus ready instantly.

"Peotor said I had another day," Boris protested.

"Peotor, my father, is no more," Vasily said, grabbing Boris by the collar and pushing him against the side of the bus. "There are no more days. This is the day to die."

Vasily, who Boris had decided the moment the young man had shot the passenger was quite insane, was sudenly on a new level of madness. It was evident in the young man's blue eyes.

With Vasily threatening, ordering, screaming, the bus was rolling down the side road near the farm ten minutes after Vasily had returned. Inside the bus were Boris, Vasily, Lia, the three others in the band, weapons piled on the seats, and a box that, Boris knew, contained explosives.

As he had on the morning Boris and the bus had been taken, Vasily stood at Boris's side. Vasily's gun was held low, out of sight of any approaching or passing vehicle. The barrel of the gun was aimed at Boris's side.

Vasily ordered Boris to drive to the right, away from the city, when they reached the main road. Vasily wanted to stay away from the store where he had made the phone call. Checking frequently with one of the members of the gang who apparently knew the local roads, Vasily prodded Boris into a series of sharp turns and down cow paths until they came to a highway.

The spot under his right armpit where the nozzle of Vasily's gun was pressed was now sore from each bump on the side roads. Boris was sweating again through his uniform.

"Can you sit down?" he asked. "You're making me—"

"Shut up and drive, drive, drive," hissed Vasily.

"I'm one of you," Boris reminded him. "Peotor said that I'm one of you. I shot the . . . I shot that man in Klin. I . . . you can trust me."

"You are a fool, bus driver," Vasily said. "My father knew you for a fool. I know you for a fool. The games have ended with you. You will drive. We will destroy the tomb, and we will all die. You understand that, bus driver? We, you, will all die. I have a list of all of our names in my pocket so they will know who we are. Your name is on that list, bus driver. My sister was to have mailed that list out of the country so the world would know. My father and sister, if they are alive, will hear what we've done and be proud." And then turning to the others in the bus, he shouted, "Today is the day we die!"

The returning shouts, Boris thought, were less than enthusiastic.

———————

Pankov, sitting behind his desk, looked up at Rostnikov, who held out the bunch of flowers.

"For your desk, Comrade Pankov," Rostnikov said. "I thought you could use a touch of color."

Pankov had not been aware that this afternoon was particularly dark, but he was pleased to have any consideration shown to him, particularly by Rostnikov, whom he liked to consider as a possible ally against the forces that threatened his security.

"Thank you, Comrade Inspector," Pankov said, rising to take the flowers. "The colonel is expecting you."

"You might want to put them in water immediately," Rostnikov suggested. "I brought them from the Arbat, and they're beginning to wilt just a bit."

Pankov grimaced slightly, retrieved a drinking glass from his desk, and hurried to the outer door.

"I'll be back instantly," he said.

"I'll explain to the colonel if he says something," said Rostnikov, and Pankov was out the door.

As quickly as his leg would allow him, Rostnikov moved around the desk, kneeled, and pulled out the bottom drawer. He reached under it and tore off the envelope in which he had placed the copies of papers he had taken from the Lentaka Shoe Factory. He closed the drawer, stood up, and was still two steps from the colonel's office door when Pankov returned, glass of water in hand.

"I ran," he said, looking at the envelope in Rostnikov's hand. Pankov was certain, or almost certain, that the inspector had entered the office with nothing but the flowers.

"I see," said Rostnikov, who knocked at the colonel's door and was told to enter.

Colonel Snitkonoy was resplendent. His uniform, the blue dress suit with all the medals, was pressed and without a speck of dust or lint. The Wolfhound's hair was neatly and recently brushed. The colonel had risen behind his desk and was pointing with his open hand at the seat across from him, which he invited Rostnikov to take. Rostnikov sat.

The afternoon was bright through the recently cleaned windows in the colonel's office. Both men paused. Just a beat. Just a moment. Just a breath. But enough for them to understand that each recognized the conversation that was about to begin would be serious.

"I've just heard from the hospital," the Wolfhound began. "Andrei Morchov is doing very well. He seems to have had an accident with a gun. Embarrassing. Comrade Morchov would prefer that very few poeple knew of this accident. I have given him every assurance of our full cooperation, and I understand our counterparts in the KGB will do the same. You understand?"

"Fully, Colonel," said Rostnikov. "There will be no report filed."

"And the investigation your staff was conducting related to Comrade Morchov is . . ." The Colonel paused.

". . . closed," said Rostnikov. "No report. It turned out to be nothing."

The Wolfhound placed his long-fingered hands on the dark wooden desk.

"You have something you wish to discuss with me, Inspector?" he said.

"I do," said Rostnikov.

"Is it something I should know or must know or would want to know?" asked the Wolfhound.

"I'll let the colonel decide," said Rostnikov, placing the envelope on top of the recently polished and highly glossed dark wooden desk.

Colonel Snitkonoy did not move. His gray eyes met Rostnikov's and paused. Without looking at the envelope, the colonel reached out and pulled it to him. He hesitated a moment and then opened the flap and pulled out the papers, laying them neatly in front of him.

While Rostnikov sat, the colonel read, slowly, carefully. At one point—and Rostnikov was sure it was when the colonel saw the name of Nahatchavanski—the Wolfhound's facade dropped for the first time in Rostnikov's memory. The colonel's hand trembled slightly. His lower lip dropped just enough to reveal even, white teeth. And then, instantly, the Wolfhound regained control and went on.

When he was finished reading the papers, the colonel looked over at Rostnikov and then proceeded to go through the papers once again. At one point while he was doing so, the phone on his desk rang. The Wolfhound ignored it.

"Badgers, ladders, and copying machines," the Wolfhound said, putting the papers back into the envelope. "You are aware, I know, of what this means, Porfiry Petrovich."

"I believe so," said Rostnikov.

"Tell me," said the colonel.

"If we turn in this evidence against a high-ranking member of the KGB we run many risks, not the least of which is the possible enmity of those in the KGB who will resent our action even if we succeed in bringing the man named in those documents to justice," said Rostnikov.

"You say 'we,' " the colonel said. "It is I who will be presenting this evidence, Inspector. Where do I say that I obtained it?"

"It came to my attention during the routine investigation of petty pilfering at the Lentaka Shoe Factory. I was completely shocked and surprised and brought it to your attention immediately."

"This could also be the pathway to new respect for our division," said the colonel. "I spoke to you recently of ambition, Porfiry Petrovich. Respect and ambition have a price. The question is: Are we willing to pay that price? I could, you know, simply turn this over to someone in the procurator's office and let them take the credit and risks."

The Wolfhound looked at Rostnikov for a long moment and made a decision.

"These medals are not simply decoration, Porfiry Petrovich," he said. "I earned them by taking chances, youthful chances, necessary chances. And when I earned them, I had the respect of those I respected. I would like to feel like that again. We will do it."

With this the colonel rose to his full height behind the desk. This was the cue for Rostnikov to rise, but he did not do so.

"There is something more, Porfiry Petrovich?" the colonel asked.

"Yes," Rostnikov said, and he proceeded to tell the Wolfhound about the death of Peotor and Sonia Kotsis and his belief that an attack on Lenin's Tomb would be made within minutes or hours.

Chapter Fourteen

Simeon Propkin, the young MVD officer guiding late-afternoon traffic crossing the bridge just below the Lenin Hills, was surprised to see the bus moving slowly in the stream of traffic. He was surprised for several reasons. First, according to the sign above the window, the bus was far off route. Though Peotor Kotsis had told him to change the route sign, Boris Trush had simply in his ongoing fear forgotten to do so. The second and perhaps more important reason Simeon Propkin, the traffic officer, was surprised was that he recognized the number of the bus as the one that had been reported missing three days earlier.

Propkin had been an active member of the MVD for only three weeks, which turned out to be fortunate, since, from the moment he saw the bus, he never considered doing anything but that which he had been told to do. Propkin let the bus pass, left his post, and hurried to the phone in his car parked in the restricted area just beyond the bridge.

"Don't speed," Vasily said as they moved away from the bridge. He punctuated his order with a sharp jab of his gun into Boris Trush's ribs.

Boris, who had been unaware that he was going too fast, slowed down.

"When we get to the square, go past the old church. If no one tries to stop you, drive slowly to the front of the tomb," Vasily said. "If someone tries to stop you, get to the tomb as fast as you can. Roll over anyone and anything in your way. You understand?"

"I understand," Boris said.

"And then," Vasily said, "we will all do our job and meet for a toast in hell."

They were less than a block from the entrance to the square when a series of events took place. The first was that a barrier had been placed across the road to the square. Boris was the first to see it. It was a yellow-and-white gate. In front of it stood two uniformed MVD men with weapons held ready across their chests. Behind the barrier stood three men, one heavyset, one young with his hair falling over his forehead, and the third tall and pale, as pale and serious as death.

Vasily saw the barrier and the men only an instant after Boris.

"Go through it," Vasily said, putting the gun to Boris's head.

"I can't," Boris said.

"You will," Vasily said, hitting Boris on the top of his head with the barrel of the gun. "You will or this bus will be painted with what little brains you have. You will because I will not fail my father and my sister. You will because this is the best moment of my life and I'll not have it screwed up by a sweating fool."

The bus was moving slowly forward. Boris could clearly see the faces of each man at the barrier. Their guns were now leveled at the window of the bus, at Boris Trush.

From somewhere behind them, within the bus, a woman's voice, Lia's, called: "Give it up, Vasily! We can't get through!"

"Shut up!" Vasily shouted, looking out the front window as the bus moved to within fifty yards of the barrier.

"We can't get through!" came another voice. Vasily let out a terrible shout, a howl of madness. He turned and fired a burst from his machine pistol into the rear of the bus. Windows exploded. Someone screamed. Boris lost control, and the bus careened to the right, hit a light pole, and came to a stop as it tilted over. Vasily tumbled toward the door, losing his grip on the gun. His head hit a window and went through it. Boris, who clung to the steering wheel in fear, reached over to open the front door with the vague thought of getting out. Behind him the terrorists screamed and shouted, and those who were uninjured and alive went through windows.

Boris let go of the steering wheel and rolled toward the door in total panic. As he went through, Vasily, his face a mask of blood, grabbed him. Boris yelped like a dog and dragged Vasily with him into the street. Boris struck at the hands that clung to him, at the face that bubbled something angry and unintelligible.

Over Vasily's shoulder as they rolled on the ground Boris could see the MVD officers and the three men behind the barrier running toward them. He struggled madly to get free of the creature who clung to him. And then Boris Trush found himself on top of Vasily Kotsis and a rush of something animallike and liberating came over him. Boris punched at the creature beneath him, the creature who was trying to strangle him with crimson, sticky fingers. Boris struck and shouted something not even he understood. He was punching furiously when the officers pulled him off the subdued man beneath him.

"Enough," said the young man with the hair in his eyes, the one who had been behind the barrier.

"Enough," Boris Trush agreed as he was led away.

His last glimpse of the scene was of the terrorists kneeling on the ground with guns trained on them and more uniformed officers rushing from doorways.

"Enough," Boris Trush repeated one more time before he passed out.

When he awakened hours later in the hospital, Boris Trush would be informed that he was a hero. And he would believe it.

Immediately after Rostnikov received the report from Karpo that the terrorists had been caught, the bus recovered, and the driver released, the inspector left for the hospital. He could return to his office later to complete the reports. A trip to the hospital would also give him time to consider how he would deal with the fact that he had interfered with a terrorism-and-hostage case that had officially been turned over to the KGB. In anticipation of an affirmative outcome to the situation, Rostnikov had already prepared a rough statement, with the Wolfhound's approval, to the effect that the colonel had simply responded to an informant who indicated that an unnamed criminal was expected to attempt a robbery not far from the Kremlin.

It was weak, but Rostnikov knew he could fill in the holes. The fact that the policeman at the bridge had called in the approach of the bus gave Rostnikov a fortunate option. Word of the approaching bus had been called in to the KGB, but since Rostnikov's people were already in the vicinity, they responded and, fortunately, were present.

It was easier to take an *elektrika* train than to try to get an automobile and a driver. Besides, the train ride gave him ample time to think.

Sarah was sitting up in bed and eating when he arrived. She was still wearing a bandage, but it was much smaller than the turban he had last seen. Her red hair was beginning to grow back.

The two other beds in the room were empty. The girl and the old woman were capable of walking and were down in the patients' dining room.

"Don't look at me," Sarah said when he came through the doorway. "I have no hair."

"It will come back," said Rostnikov, moving to her side to kiss her cheek. "What are you eating?"

"I don't know," she said, looking down at the tray on her lap. "It's wet, white, and has lumps of something in it. Would you like some?"

"No, thank you," he said, resting on the side of her bed. "What does the doctor say today?"

"Three, four more days and I can go home," she said. She handed him the tray, and he put it on the table nearby. "Porfiry, why have we not heard from Iosef?"

"He's all right," he said, taking her hand. "I'll find out tonight or tomorrow. I'll talk to him."

"It's not a good experience, the army," she said, looking at him.

"One can learn from it," said Rostnikov. "There is no war now. It's just boredom, routine, and stupidity."

"Yes," she said, making it evident that she did not believe him. "Ivan Bulgarin, have you found him? How is he?"

"No," said Rostnikov, remembering the man who walked like a bear. "But I think we need have no fear about his well-being."

"I'm not so certain," she said. "You know, I thought I was going to die in here."

"I know," he said.

"I didn't want to think about the future," she went on, holding tightly to his rough hand. "Now we should think about the future again."

"And what shall we think?" he asked.

She said nothing and he understood. She was dreaming of leaving the Soviet Union.

"I'm tired again, Porfiry," she said. "Those pills they give me."

"Sleep," he said, getting up from the bed. "I'll be back tomorrow."

"Don't forget to eat, Porfiry," she said dreamily.

"I won't," he promised.

And instantly she was asleep or pretending to be.

It was raining gently when Rostnikov stepped out of the hospital. There was a chance, if he moved quickly, that he could catch the ten o'clock train back to Moscow. He was not at all sure he could move quickly, but as it turned out, he did not have to hurry, nor did he have to take the train.

―――――――

When Sasha Tkach reached home that evening, he was greeted at the door by Maya and Pulcharia. Maya kissed him, closed the door, and handed him the baby, who leaned over quickly to give his nose a toothless, moist, and gentle bite.

"Is Lydia home?" he asked.

"Yes," Maya said. "And she is in a good mood. She says she is looking forward now to the move. And she is going out tonight. I think Lydia has a date."

"Lydia has . . ." Sasha said.

Pulcharia tried to poke a finger in his eye, but Sasha turned his head and moved to the chair in the corner of the room.

"Yes," Maya said. "She . . . What's wrong?"

The tired smile on Sasha's face had disappeared. His eyes had fallen on the table, set for dinner and containing a small glass in which were nestled the flowers he had given to Lydia so long ago that morning, the flowers of Sonia Kotsis, who had shot off the top of her head in front of Sasha Tkach.

Sasha clutched the baby close to him, closed his eyes, and felt Maya's hand on his head. In the next room, Lydia Tkach burst into a loud and off-key version of something that may have been "Waltzing Matilda."

Sasha wept.

Stuart M. Kaminsky

Emil Karpo ate a dinner of bread and herring while working at the desk in his room. He drank mineral water and carefully completed his notes on both the Morchov case and his part in the apprehension of Vasily Kotsis and the rescue of the bus driver. He had written official reports at Petrovka and checked the pending investigations file. On the way to his apartment he had made a slight detour to confront the meat dealer whose name he had been given. The man, standing alone in a small room behind his small shop inches from the pale policeman, had been most cooperative. Karpo was certain that by the next morning he would have in his custody the men who had been kidnapping pets.

He finished his food, cleared away each crumb carefully, packed his small garbage, and walked it down to the trash room on the first floor.

It was still early when Karpo returned to his room, took off his jacket and shoes, and sat on the floor to meditate. For a moment he thought he felt the aura of a migraine headache, but it did not come, and he felt a pang of disappointment, for in spite of the pain, the headaches were old acquaintances.

Porfiry Petrovich had recently suggested to Karpo that the headaches may have been his body's way of forcing Karpo to relax, to pay attention to his bodily needs. Yes, Karpo thought, remembering his recent conversation with Rostnikov. The machine is not a human body, and the human body is not a machine.

The Man Who Walked Like a Bear

Emil sat on the floor and crossed his legs, focused on a whorl in the wood of his chair, and found himself imagining Yuri and Jalna alone in the dacha, huddled together with new hope and the specter of murder lifted from them. Karpo refocused, trying to turn the image to white, but the image of the two young people alone, laughing in bed, would not go away.

Karpo rose from the floor. It was a week early. He had never violated his schedule, had never given in to the animal needs of his body, though he never denied them. But this need he felt was without words and beyond his understanding.

He would explore it, control it, but first he had to give it what it demanded. Karpo put on his jacket and shoes and left his room. He ignored the light rain and found a phone. He placed his call and waited.

"Mathilde Verson," he said to the man who answered the phone. Behind the man he could hear soft jazz music. And then he heard her voice.

"Yes?" she said.

"It's me," said Karpo.

"What can I do for you, Emil?" she asked. "You need some information?"

"No," he said. "I would like to see you. Are you . . . available?"

"It's not Thursday," she said. "Are you all right?"

"Yes."

"I'm available," she said.

"I'll be there in fifteen minutes," he said and hung up the phone.

It was done. He had no idea what he would tell her. All he knew was that for the first time in his life he did not want to be alone.

The car that pulled up beside Rostnikov on the rain-deserted street near the hospital was large, dark, and not very old. The rear door opened. Rostnikov could see no one inside, but he recognized the invitation and it was not completely unexpected. The rain had begun to fall harder. Rostnikov moved to the car and slid in next to Schroeder, the hospital administrator. Schroeder glanced at Rostnikov, who closed the door as the driver moved quickly away from the curb.

"You made a mistake, Comrade Inspector," Schroeder said without looking at Rostnikov. "You should have been looking for me in the hospital. You should have asked more questions about Ivan Bulgarin. You are in trouble."

Rostnikov grunted. He had made no mistake.

"Why did you stop looking for Bulgarin?" Schroeder asked conversationally.

And Rostnikov understood. It was Schroeder who had made the mistake, Schroeder who had failed to keep Rostnikov looking for Ivan Bulgarin. It was Schroeder who was in trouble.

"Ivan Bulgarin did not need my help," Rostnikov said.

Neither man spoke again for the remainder of the ride. Schroeder looked out of his window and Rostnikov out of his as the rain quickened and the sound of the windshield wiper lulled.

The car stopped before the door to Lubyanka, KGB headquarters. The rain had slowed a bit. Rostnikov stepped out and looked back across the square at the statue of Felix Dzerzinsky, father of the Soviet secret police. Schroeder joined him, and the car pulled away.

The policeman and the KGB man walked to the door and entered. On either side of the dank entryway stood a uniformed and armed guard, who watched as the two men approached the desk in front of them. The woman behind the desk looked at Schroeder, who displayed an identification card, and then at Rostnikov, who removed his identification card and handed it to the woman. She placed the card on a thin metal plate on the corner of the desk and pressed a white button next to the plate. There was a slight hum, and the woman returned Rostnikov's card without a word.

The rest of the journey was a familiar one to Porfiry Petrovich. Schroeder moved slowly, allowing Rostnikov to keep pace with him. Rostnikov was sure, however, that Schroeder was not slowing his pace out of concern for the policeman. Schroeder was in no hurry to get where they were going. Up one stairway, down the corridor, and then what he had suspected was confirmed. They stopped in front of a dark, heavy wooden door. Schroeder hesitated and then knocked.

The door opened and a powerful-looking giant of a man in his late thirties stepped back to let them in. The powerful man wore a dark blue suit. He was clean-shaven with hair blond and cut short, and he looked very like the last man who had opened this door for Rostnikov.

The powerful man moved across the small carpeted room furnished with three chairs against the wall, a desk with a chair, and a single photograph of Lenin on the wall. The man knocked gently at the far door, and a voice Rostnikov recognized called, "Send him in, Vadim."

The powerful man opened the door, and Rostnikov stepped forward. Vadim Schroeder hesitated, considered entering with him, and thought better of it. The door was closed gently behind him by the powerful man when Rostnikov entered the room and found himself facing the KGB officer, Colonel Zhenya.

Zhenya was no more than forty-five, very young for one of such rank. He had moved up when his predecessor, who was not a young man, died after a long and painful illness. Zhenya, immaculate, thin, balding, and dark, wore his uniform, a uniform devoid of decoration. For an instant Rostnikov looked at the man seated behind the desk with folded hands, the barred window, the uniform, and the sparseness of the room and wondered if Zhenya had created a prison for himself.

"Sit, Rostnikov," Zhenya said.

Rostnikov sat. The rain brushed against the window loudly and then went back to its steady drum.

Whatever Zhenya wanted, Rostnikov was sure, would not come directly or quickly. It was a game both men had played throughout their lives. Zhenya had started the game. Now he would have to make the first move.

"You interfered with a KGB operation this morning," Zhenya said, unclasping his hands and putting a finger on a dark, thick file folder on the desk. "The Turkistani business could have had disastrous consequences as a result of your ego."

"I will submit a complete report by morning, Comrade Colonel," Rostnikov said. "The presence of my colleagues at the square was coincidental."

"A fortunate coincidence," said Zhenya with a smile that was not a smile.

"Full credit belongs to Colonel Snitkonoy," said Rostnikov.

"Yes, I understand he will be properly rewarded for his quick thinking and the efficiency of his staff," said Zhenya. "He had a very busy, a very productive day."

The pause was long. The two men listened to the rain.

"Do you know why you are here, Rostnikov?" Zhenya said.

"Nahatchavanski," said Rostnikov.

"Yes," said Zhenya. "Nahatchavanski. That will get your colonel a promotion, more responsibility. And with that come enemies. Your colonel has long been considered a harmless buffoon. Since you have joined his staff, he has become more formidable. I doubt you have done him a service, Rostnikov."

"I do my duty," Rostnikov said.

"Why did you stop looking for Ivan Bulgarin?" said Zhenya.

It was time. Rostnikov's move.

"There is no Ivan Bulgarin," said Rostnikov.

"When did you know this?" asked Zhenya.

"I suspected from the start," said Rostnikov. "The naked giant who entered my wife's room and whispered a cryptic clue to corruption was well staged but a bit coincidental. The mental ward of the hospital is in a far wing. He had to wander a long distance and randomly select the room in which a policeman happened to be visiting."

"You were not sure," said Zhenya.

"No," said Rostnikov. "Not then."

"You are a suspicious man, Rostnikov."

"One has to be to survive," Rostnikov said with a shrug. "May I rise?"

"If you must," said Zhenya.

Rostnikov rose slowly, bent his left leg, and rubbed the knee.

"Are you in pain, Rostnikov?"

"One learns to live with discomfort, Colonel, even pain."

"What confirmed your suspicion?"

"Not the car you had following me," said Rostnikov, sitting again. "That could have been for a variety of reasons, but it was on the heels of the Bulgarin incident. You made it too easy, Colonel."

Zhenya could not keep his back from going straight at the insult, but he let nothing show on his face.

"Easy," Zhenya repeated.

"Lukov, the Lentaka Shoe Factory manager, was too nervous," Rostnikov went on. "But that could well have been a natural fear of the police. And then he gave up the name of Nahatchavanski too quickly, too easily. Yet that, too, could have been. The papers were too easy to find. It is difficult to believe that a man with the experience of General Nahatchavanski would allow papers that would incriminate him to be left in the files of a shoe factory."

"Yes," Zhenya agreed. "It was too easy, but I had no time for great subtlety. The longer you took, the more likely Nahatchavanski would discover your investigation and, possibly, trace it back to me. What other errors did my staff make? I would like to profit from this experience."

"It was not difficult to notice the car that followed us the night we broke into the factory," said Rostnikov. "Whoever was in that car should have made a pretense at least of searching my apartment, my office, that of my men in case they were seen."

"Then, Inspector, why did you let us lead you along?"

"Because," Rostnikov answered, "General Nahatcha-vanski is guilty."

There were things that now were better left unsaid. Clearly, Zhenya had used Rostnikov to further his own career and rid himself of an enemy without risking an attack on a fellow KGB officer, an officer who, Rostnikov assumed, he wished to replace. And it was now clear that Rostnikov had used Zhenya to catch a high-ranking criminal within the ranks of the KGB.

"Have you considered the possibility that you may not leave this building?" asked Zhenya.

"Yes, Colonel," Rostnikov said, looking at the window. The rain had stopped, and there was only darkness. "When I turned over to Colonel Snitkonoy the copy of the papers I had taken from the Lentaka Shoe Factory, I also gave him a report indicating the suspicions I have just related to you. The report also suggested that the apprehension of the general would not have been possible without the aid of cooperative individuals with the KGB. I named no names, for I had none, but I think it would not be difficult to determine who those cooperative individuals are. And, I suspect, if I disappear, the colonel will swiftly pursue the possibilities for my disappearance suggested by my report."

Zhenya stood, walked to the window, and looked out, though there was nothing he could possibly have seen in the darkness. He put his hands behind his back and turned to Rostnikov.

"This is a dangerous game, Rostnikov," Zhenya warned.

"For both of us, Colonel. You can rely upon my silence. There is nothing for me in attempting to implicate you."

"You want something more, Rostnikov. I want your silence. You want your safety, but you want more," said Zhenya, moving back to this desk.

"My wife and I would like to leave the Soviet Union," Rostnikov said.

"Impossible," replied Zhenya.

"I know," said Rostnikov. "But I will settle for the release of my son from the army. He has served his time."

Iosef Rostnikov's military service had twice been extended, including an extension during the Afghanistan campaign. The reason given was the need for Iosef's special skills, skills that had never been utilized by the military. The real reason Iosef Rostnikov was kept in the army was to keep his safety as a sword over the head of his troublesome father.

"I will inquire," said Zhenya.

"I would be grateful for any assistance you can give, Colonel," said Rostnikov.

"I don't like you, Rostnikov," Zhenya said. "That, I am sure, comes as no surprise to you. You are hampered by a sense of justice at odds with the goals of the State. You interfere, Rostnikov, and you believe that because you are good at what you do you will survive. You will not survive, Rostnikov."

Zhenya's words had been delivered, beginning to end, in an emotionless monotone. Rostnikov nodded when he was finished. The colonel pulled the files on his desk in front of him, adjusted his glasses, and began to read. Rostnikov was being dismissed and ignored.

Porfiry Petrovich Rostnikov got up and moved to the door. He opened it and stepped into the small office, where he found the giant standing with his arms folded. Vadim Schroeder was gone.

Rostnikov did not stare at the huge man who lumbered slowly like a bear to open the outer door, beyond which Schroeder stood waiting to lead Rostnikov through the labyrinth of Lubyanka. The giant's blue eyes met those of Rostnikov, and it was clear that the policeman recognized the man he had known briefly as Ivan Bulgarin. The giant smiled slightly as he closed the door behind the inspector.

Schroeder led the way through the building without speaking. When they reached the front entrance, Schroeder opened the door and said, "The car will take you home."

"Thank you," said Rostnikov.

"Your discussion with the colonel went well?" Schroeder said as Rostnikov went down the stone steps and headed for the waiting, humming automobile.

"Yes," said Rostnikov.

Schroeder stood on the step wanting to ask more, wanting a clue to his own future, but he dared not ask. Rostnikov climbed into the car and settled back. He was very tired.

Back in his apartment, Rostnikov ate some bread and drank the last of a jar of potato soup. Slowly he undressed, put on his sweatshirt, pulled his bench and weights out of the cabinet in the corner of the living room, and turned on the record player.

Then to the sound of Edith Piaf softly singing of a lost love, Rostnikov lost himself in the magic of two-handed curls.

———

Three nights and one day later, Porfiry Petrovich Rostnikov opened the door of Sarah's room at the September 1947

Hospital. She was ready for him in the wheelchair. Her lips were touched with pink, and the bandages had been removed. Her freshly combed hair seemed to have lost just a shade of its redness, but it may simply, Rostnikov thought, be my memory. Sarah was wearing her pink-and-white robe and her matching pink slippers.

The other two beds in the room were occupied by new patients, one covered and asleep and with a tuft of white hair, the other a thin woman of perhaps forty who looked at Rostnikov over half glasses.

"Do I look . . . ?" Sarah said.

"You look fine," said Rostnikov, moving to kiss her forehead.

"You lie, Porfiry Petrovich," she said with a sigh.

"When I must, but not to you," he said. "Dr. Yegeneva says we can go to the roof."

"It looks as if it might be a little cold," said Sarah as Rostnikov got behind the chair and pushed her toward the door he had left open. "Winter's coming."

"Yes," he said, wheeling her slowly down the hall, the wheels clicking in need of oil, Rostnikov's leg struggling to keep the movement even.

"And that makes you happy," she went on as they reached the elevator. Rostnikov pushed the button and stood before her.

"I like the winter," he said.

"How much time can you spend with me today?" she asked, touching her hair with a pale hand.

"All day. Till you tire."

The elevator opened. It was empty. Rostnikov pushed the wheelchair in and hit the button to close the door.

As the elevator moved up the two floors to the roof,

Rostnikov asked, "I have a surprise. Are you able to take a surprise?"

Sarah looked up at her husband, saw the small smile, and knew there was no terror in the surprise. She looked at his hands, but they held nothing.

"Yes," she said.

And then the elevator door opened. There was a double door to the roof in front of them. The door was open. The fall wind blew and hummed and Sarah savored it and felt her body under its touch and was glad to be alive. As Rostnikov wheeled her around a corner onto the open roof, she reached up to touch his hand.

It was at that moment that she saw the sturdy, smiling young man standing no more than ten paces in front of her. He wore dark trousers and a black knit turtleneck sweater she had bought him for his last birthday.

"He can stay, Sarah," Rostnikov said, squeezing her hand gently. "He is no longer a soldier."

Iosef moved forward to his mother, and Porfiry pretended not to hear the sob that came from the soul of his wife.